Irresistible Ink

Inked in the Steel City Book 6

RANAE ROSE

Irresistible Ink

This book is a work of fiction. All characters, names, places and events are products of the author's imagination and are in no way real. Any resemblance to real events or persons, living or dead, is entirely coincidental.

Cover photo by: Michael Stokes

ISBN: 1497559979
ISBN-13: 978-1497559974

CONTENTS

CHAPTER 1

James was already halfway in love with Arianna. How could he not be? She was like a goddess in his tattoo chair. The rest of the Hot Ink Tattoo Studio had faded into the background, a blur of light and noise and things he didn't – couldn't – give a damn about as long as she was there. He couldn't have said what song was playing on the radio, or how many other clients were in the shop, if his life had depended on it. And he'd been going like this for hours.

For some clients, he would've suggested breaking a tattoo like Arianna's latest down into more than one session. Not for his own sake, but to reduce the pain and keep the client from having to sit still and bear it for so long. Not Arianna Valencia.

This was the third tattoo he'd done for her, and he knew she'd sit still as a statue, a model client as he worked. She was as silent as a statue, too – maybe too quiet.

Pausing to lift excess ink from her skin with a clean cloth, he allowed himself to glance up at her face for a few glorious seconds while the blue cotton absorbed the mess.

Damn, she was beautiful. Every time he saw her, the first thing he noticed was her eyes – big and greenish-brown, with tiny golden flecks. They were set off by her warm olive skin and full lips, which she'd painted with a translucent gloss the color of ripe cherries. She'd pulled her dark brown waves back into a messy ponytail to make sure they stayed out of the way while he worked, tattooing her upper left arm, but he could recall exactly how they framed her face when they were free.

He was pretty sure she was Latina, mixed heritage probably, though he couldn't be more specific than that. He couldn't say where eyes like that had come from, because he'd never seen any quite like them. The same went for the rest of her features.

She shifted her gaze, and when her eyes locked with his, he felt like he'd been electrified somewhere in the very center of his chest, beneath his breastbone. "Is everything all right?" she asked.

"Yeah." He tore his gaze away from her face, focusing again on the tattoo he'd poured hours into. "Almost done. How are you holding up?"

"Fine."

She said the same thing every time he asked.

"Okay. Don't be afraid to say so if you want to stop for a break."

She nodded, and his heart deflated a little. Every time she came in, he made sure to leave time in his schedule for breaks, and he could never help fantasizing about how he might charm her during those times, if she ever decided to take one. They could get coffee across the street. Hell, anything. But she always sat resolutely through the session, glossy lips frozen in a natural pout that had nothing to do with emotion.

Some of his clients talked his ear off. She wasn't one of them. In fact, she never really spoke unless spoken to – a fact that left him wishing he could come up with more interesting things to say. He didn't exactly have the gift of gab either, and God knew there'd been times when he'd prayed silently for some clients to shut up – especially some women around Arianna's age who blabbed on about their boyfriends or other overly-personal crap. He wasn't a freaking hairdresser; he didn't gossip, or offer his inexpert insight on relationship woes. And yet…

He would've given his left nut to hear Arianna confide in him. Her quiet demeanor combined with his lust made her appealingly mysterious, and he probably would've lapped up anything she would've told him about herself. And then he would've used it to try to establish some sort of connection between them – something more than ink and blood and the unique magic forged by the art she trusted him to apply to her body. That was special and all, but he was interested in a hell of a lot more than that.

As she remained silent, the buzz of his tattoo machine provided a steady hum, an undercurrent of noise to his equally persistent and focused thoughts. The tattoo captivated him simply because Arianna was the canvas, sure, but beyond that, it was on par with his best work. As he finished the colorful design with a few last touches of crimson, he was proud of what he'd done … proud to have added something so beautiful to such a perfect body.

A few minutes later, he gently blotted the last of the extra ink from her skin, using a cloth to absorb a drop of crimson that had welled up beneath one of the skull's eye sockets, like a tear of blood. Maybe it was a morbid notion, but the tattoo was anything but. Outlined in heavy black, vibrantly colored and framed by two small marigold blossoms, the sugar skull design was both strong and beautiful, bold and delicate, just like Arianna.

There was no question – the design suited her.

"Well?" After cleaning the tattoo, he turned her chair so that she'd be able to see her new ink clearly in his booth's mirror.

She studied her reflection silently, eyes shining in the clear lighting.

Standing behind her chair with his hands resting on the back of it, on either side of her shoulders, James was uncharacteristically nervous. He knew the tattoo was good, but he needed to hear her say it. She didn't usually say much at all, but he wanted to know her thoughts – wanted to know she liked it as much as he did.

"It looks great," she said, meeting his eyes in the mirror. "Just like I imagined. Thank you."

Standing there looming over her almost-bare shoulders – she wore a cami with thin straps – and resisting the urge to stare down at her cleavage, he was half-hard. His dick swelled a little larger against his jeans as her approval registered, and he knew he had it bad.

"Zoe will make sure you have a sheet printed with aftercare instructions when you leave. I'm sure you know the drill by now, but the basics are…" He went over them with her anyway, not ready to watch her walk away. The tattoo was done – who knew when, if ever, he'd see her again?

He couldn't just let her leave this time. The first couple times he'd tattooed her, he hadn't had the balls to ask her out. She was hard to read, and he hadn't wanted to offend a client – especially one he really wanted to see again. Now, though…

There was no way in hell he could just let her slip through his fingers. He had to at least give it a shot. Bandaging her tattoo, he focused on her arm, the vibrant ink disappearing beneath a layer of sterile gauze. "So, you headed home after this?"

"Yeah."

Even her monosyllabic reply turned him on. Where did she call home – did she live alone? He would've liked to know. Plus, it was kind of hot to picture her skipping around an otherwise empty apartment in a lot less than the jeans and cami she wore now. Not that she seemed the skipping type, really, but hell...

His gaze was drawn irresistibly to the V of smooth cleavage displayed by her top. Her breasts weren't huge, but they'd each be a perfect handful.

"Me too," he said. "You're my only appointment today, other than a piercing I did before you came in." That hadn't taken long. He purposely hadn't scheduled any other tattoos for the day, wanting to devote all his time and energy to the lengthy session hers had needed.

"What kind of piercing was it?"

He snapped his gaze up to meet hers. A question, from Arianna? And she seemed genuinely interested. Why, God, did this have to be the one subject she wanted to talk about?

"Nipple," he replied. "Two nipple piercings."

Her expression didn't betray much.

"My client was a guy," he added. "Don't see what he wanted the nipple rings for – he had so much hair on his chest that you could hardly see them. But whatever."

Her cherry-red lips quirked in a silent smile, and that made the hairy nipple-piercing experience worth it.

"That sounds like it would hurt like hell," she said.

James nodded, unable to resist letting his gaze sweep over the double-swells of her breasts. Just wondering what color her nipples were made his mouth water.

"It does." Most of his clients reported that nipple piercings were definitely painful. Knowing Arianna, she probably wouldn't make a sound if it were her. And what a thought that was…

His dick shifted painfully against the fly of his jeans as he imagined placing his hands on her breasts, driving hard metal through soft flesh. Normally, he viewed his piercing work with a clinical practicality – how else was a guy supposed to go about a job that involved handling strangers' intimate body parts, including other guys' hairy nipples, or even their dicks?

Just the thought of Arianna peeling down one of her cami straps and exposing a breast threatened to take his breath away, though. Good thing she'd never expressed any interest in body piercing.

"I've considered maybe getting a piercing," she said.

James nearly choked, on absolutely nothing at all.

"My nose – a stud in one nostril."

He drew a deep breath, gaze flickering up to her beautiful face as he envisioned a tiny jewel nestled in the little crease above the flare of one perfectly-shaped nostril. "It'd look good on you. If you ever decide you want to do it, just give me a call. We'll set up an appointment."

She nodded, slowly, looking like she actually might do just that.

Damn if that didn't serve as a temptation to let her go now, to tell himself that she'd be back, and that he'd wait until then to make his move…

But no – he'd waited long enough. "About today. Can I take you out? For dinner, coffee or something."

He bit his tongue, tasting a hint of blood as he realized he had a death grip on the tattoo chair Arianna still sat in. His heart beat hard, sending more blood surging below his belt as she met his eyes in the mirror. "You mean like a date?"

* * * * *

"Yeah, a date." James Layton's voice was a little deep, a little rough – the stuff of fantasies. His eyes – a murky grey-green Arianna had noticed a million times before – remained locked with hers as she returned his gaze in the mirror.

She sat frozen, gripping the arms of the tattoo chair so hard she wouldn't have been surprised if the tips of her nails had broken off. She took the time to swallow, doing her best to get rid of the feeling that her heart was in her throat. "Sure."

Fireworks erupted in some dark corner of her consciousness, dazzling her with the possibilities that had just opened up. Accepting his invitation was a no-brainer, but saying yes still gave her a thrill and left her more than a little nervous.

James was hot. Way too hot to turn down, with his short blond hair, chiseled cheekbones and chiseled … everything. He wore jeans and a t-shirt, but the muscles in his arms were clearly defined beneath ink that looked natural on him, the various designs like a patina brought on by time and experience – a life lived fully, so far, she imagined.

That was what her own new tattoo was about: a celebration of life. A life she was determined to start living more fully, to be specific. She'd told herself she wanted to step out of her shell more, so why not start embracing life by embracing James? God knew she'd fantasized about him a million times since the first time he'd tattooed her.

"Great," he said, still leaning over her chair, still holding her gaze. "Where do you want to go?"

"Dinner would be nice." She was hungry. Up until he'd asked her out, her evening plans had included going home, rustling up some leftovers and fitting in a couple hours of work before zoning out in front of the TV, or maybe her e-reader.

This was going to be so much better than the lame, solitary hours she'd planned. As James finally straightened, removing his hands from the chair and breaking eye contact, a bolt of longing went right through the center of her being, perilously close to her heart.

As she stood too, shrugging into a light sweater and picking up her purse, she did her best to brush the feeling off. It wasn't like she expected the world from James. She didn't expect anything more than what he'd offered: a date, and if the look in his eyes was any indication, one that'd be just as hot as he was. It would be fun, and it'd been about a million years since she'd been foolish enough to expect anything more than that from anyone.

"There's a place I've been waiting for an excuse to try out," he said.

She lifted her gaze and was instantly locked in eye contact that made her heart speed. "Perfect."

He was. And the evening would be too, as long as she remembered not to take it too seriously.

* * * * *

The restaurant offered a river view that was romantic as hell. The close quarters also meant that James and Arianna were both practically straddling each other's thighs as they sat at a tiny two-person table.

Perfect. Now James knew why Tyler had told him he should try the place next time he had a date. He'd have to thank him later. For now, though, he focused on the firm, warm pressure of Arianna's leg against his. The tablecloth hid an erection he didn't bother trying to fight.

"So what's good here?" Arianna asked, opening her menu. "Oh, that's right – this is your first time too. Never mind."

He struggled to give his menu more than a cursory glance – Arianna was so much more appealing to look at. When the server arrived to take their orders, he chose the first item that caught his eye.

"That sounds good," Arianna said. "I'll try it too."

James glanced back down at his menu just as the waiter whisked it away. Hopefully the seared steak with caramelized onions and gorgonzola was good. And hopefully it wouldn't make his breath reek. He hadn't thought of that when he'd rattled off his choice, and now it was too late.

"So how long have you been tattooing at Hot Ink?" Arianna asked, breaking her characteristic silence.

James watched her lips move, imagining them crushed against his. Thank God her question was one that didn't require much thought. "Seven years. Jed took me on as an apprentice when I was 21. Been there ever since."

So much had changed since those early days that they seemed a million years ago. James' life had been a black hole: empty and uncharted. Working at Hot Ink had given it shape and meaning. Jed had generously mentored him, keeping him on as an apprentice even after his wife and Hot Ink co-founder, Alice, died.

Even on the days Jed had been too crippled by grief to make an appearance, James had been glad to answer the phone and keep the shop clean. As someone who'd spent most of his life having nothing, Hot Ink had quickly become everything to him.

"We're almost the same age," Arianna said. "I'm 26." She smiled briefly, looking almost shy, then clamed up.

Several silent seconds slipped by, and James sensed that she'd really put herself out on a limb by starting the small talk. "What about you?" he hurried to ask, eager to keep the conversation from drying up. "What do you do?"

He had no idea what she did for a living. With most repeat clients, he would've known already.

"I'm a graphic designer. Freelance."

"So you design what – websites and stuff?"

"Not exactly. Advertisements. Logos. Web graphics. I've done a lot of different stuff. Even some book covers."

James' gaze was drawn to her arms. They were covered by a light button-up sweater she'd pulled on back at Hot Ink, but he could see every swirl of ink beneath with perfect clarity in his mind's eye. "I'm not surprised. You have an eye for design."

Her lips curled in a sudden smile that reached all the way to the corners of her eyes, creating tiny crinkles. Seeing her expression transform that way made him feel invincible. His confidence stoked, he forged ahead. "I bet your work kicks ass. Did you go to school or learn on your own?"

Her smile flickered. "I did go to school. Graduated from Carnegie Mellon a few years ago. But..."

That was impressive. James told her so, ignoring the stabbing jolt of inadequacy that slipped between his ribs, knocking his confidence down a notch. So what if Arianna was out of his league? He'd known that the moment he'd laid eyes on her. She was the kind of woman that was more or less out of any man's league – unbelievably beautiful. The fact that she was educated on top of it wasn't going to stop him from pursuing her. Not now that he'd gotten her here and she was practically straddling his thigh beneath the table.

He'd never finished highschool. At least, not in the normal way. He'd gone back later and gotten his GED. Luckily, she didn't ask about that.

"My education is more impressive than my actual work, I guess." She frowned, tipping her head to the side.

"Why do you say that?" She was doing something she liked and something she was good at. It made sense to him.

Was he too ignorant to see why she should be doing anything else?

She shrugged. "My family imagined me making waves and climbing ladders in corporate America after graduating from college, I guess. Or at least holding down a modest traditional job. Instead I bought myself a new laptop loaded with editing and design programs and started churning out pretty graphics from a desk in one corner of my apartment."

"So you're an artist instead of a cubicle slave. That sounds like a good thing to me, but maybe I'm biased."

After a moment's hesitation, she smiled again.

When their food arrived, it introduced a natural lull to the conversation. He didn't mind. Arianna had already said more to him while they'd waited than she had during all three of their tattoo sessions combined. It seemed like a good start.

By the time they finished eating, it felt like more than a good start. It felt like the start of what he'd been aching for ever since the first time he'd laid eyes on her. She still wasn't what he'd call easy to read, but he had a feeling … a feeling that resonated in every fiber of his being, including the rock-hard length of his dick, which throbbed against his jeans zipper as he watched her touch her tongue to her lower lip, obliterating a drop of chocolate sauce her dessert had left behind.

"Listen," he said after he'd paid for their dinner and they'd left the restaurant, "we've still got the whole night ahead of us. Our date doesn't have to end here if you're having a good time."

Forget the river view the restaurant had offered; she was beautiful, and he couldn't drag his gaze away from her face as they stood by his car, his words hanging in the air between them.

Her gaze drifted south slowly, and he all but felt it burning over his body, resting for a moment on his jeans, just below the hem of his t-shirt. The May evening air was cool, if the way her nipples pricked against her top – two small buds that made his mouth water – was any indication.

He didn't feel even a hint of cold. In fact, his blood might as well have been hot lava.

He knew she could see that he was hard, knew the ache in his groin meant his lust was outlined beneath the inadequate cover of denim. He didn't try to hide it. He couldn't have if he'd wanted to, for one. And if there was a chance that she wanted what he lusted for, he was more than willing to lay his intentions out on the line.

CHAPTER 2

"I'm having a good time," Arianna finally said, her fingertips drifting to brush the handle of his car's passenger-side door. "I don't have any plans for the rest of the evening, either."

Heart speeding, James reached out and slipped his hand over hers, opening the door for her. "Let me take you to my place instead of taking you home, then."

He lived alone. Empty and quiet, his apartment was more than ready to accommodate a date for a few hours or a night – however long she'd stay.

For a moment, her glossed lips remained sealed, and she looked just like she had sitting in his tattoo chair. "Okay."

He'd never been so glad to hear one of her short replies. As he helped her into the car and rounded the front of the vehicle, settling behind the wheel, he felt his lust for her all the way down in his bones. Would she have said yes if he'd asked her out sooner, after one of their first two sessions? Thinking of what he might've been missing out on physically hurt.

But there was no telling, and whatever the answer was, he was glad it was happening now. So glad that his balls were hugging his body, aching against the seat as he brought the engine to life and steered the car for his place. They'd left her vehicle behind in the lot near Hot Ink – they'd worry about that later. Right now, he had a one-track mind. Instinct and familiarity guided him home, leading him to take turns he barely thought about, eventually reaching his apartment.

Arianna let him take her hand as he helped her out of the car. Afterward, he held on. Kind of weird that this was the first time he'd laid hands on her, outside of his tattoo booth. They were just minutes away from doing things he'd been fantasizing about for months, and they'd only now gotten so far as hand holding. When he finally touched her in the privacy of his apartment, it'd be a rush – almost too much, except he knew he'd never get too much of her. The thought made his head spin and his cock throb.

"This one's mine," he said, nodding toward a unit on the ground floor. 116 – a one bedroom apartment and home sweet home for the past three years.

"This one?" Arianna's question resonated as they approached the unit.

"Yeah…" He stopped a few steps away from the door as a feeling of wrongness registered. He blinked as he double-checked the number on the door, then looked back down at what was taking up just about all the space on the tiny stoop.

What. The. Fuck?

"Um." Arianna stood motionless beside him, her hand still caught up inside one of his. "Do you have a kid? Because there's a car seat on your doorstep."

"No." His heart crept into his throat, the thought almost choking him. A kid? He didn't have any family he was close enough to so much as share a phone call with, let alone a child. "My neighbor has a baby. Maybe she left it here by mistake."

14

Why anyone would leave a car seat sitting outside, exposed to the elements, was beyond him, but whatever. That was his neighbor's business and the only thing he cared about right now was getting Arianna inside. Reaching down, he lifted the car seat, setting it aside in the empty space between his unit and 118.

Except when he went to let go, he couldn't. Shock froze his fingers around the handle as he caught a glimpse of the seat's interior. Cradled in the safety harness and bundled up to its chin in a fuzzy yellow blanket, there was a baby.

A live, human baby. Alone. On his doorstep. It was so unbelievably tiny he might've thought it was a doll – some kind of joke – but it sneezed.

He almost dropped the car seat. Almost. Catching himself at the last second, he knelt down instead, getting a close look at the kid, as if that would make the situation any less weird.

"This isn't my kid," he said, realizing that he'd let go of Arianna's hand and hoping she hadn't turned tail and fled.

"Then whose is it?" Her voice came from surprisingly close by, her breath warming his ear as she crouched down beside him.

"I don't know."

She reached out and pulled something he hadn't even noticed from the doorstep – a cheap vinyl bag printed with daisies and cartoon elephants. "Here's a diaper bag," she said. "But where's the mother?"

She looked around and James joined her, tearing his gaze away from the little round face that didn't belong anywhere near his doorstep.

The parking lot was empty, except for a guy who loitered near one of the farthest spaces, leaning up against a nineties model sedan.

"Hey," James called, rising. "You know who this kid belongs to?"

The man opened the driver's side door without answering.

"Hey!" James called out, louder. "Did you see the mother? Is she around?"

The man moved with surprising speed, practically leaping into the car. As a sense of suspicion crept up on James, the car peeled out of the parking lot, swerving dangerously and disappearing down the street.

"Well, I think we know who left the baby on your doorstep."

James stood, dumbstruck, trying to remember everything he could about the man who'd probably abandoned the baby. Tall, brown hair. Twenties, maybe thirties? Already, the details were beginning to fade. "What the hell?"

The baby squirmed, releasing a wail that sounded too loud to have come from its tiny lungs. Guilt crept over James as he realized he'd sworn in front of the kid. Was feeling bad about it stupid? It wasn't like it could understand. Hell, it looked like it had literally been born yesterday.

James' anxiety rose with each passing second as the kid screamed like an air raid siren. The sound was like nails on a chalk board, a cry that demanded something be done. But what? He couldn't just whisk some stranger's baby inside his apartment, and he didn't know what to do to make it stop crying anyway.

Arianna reached out and unbuckled the car seat's harness with surprising dexterity, lifting the bundle of blankets into her arms.

James couldn't help but admire her in the same way he might've admired someone handling a wild, potentially dangerous animal. An alligator wrestler or snake charmer, maybe.

The baby stopped crying the instant she cradled it against her chest, arms crossing protectively over the little body swathed in pastel blankets. Unfortunately, the silence only lasted for a second.

"She's hungry," Arianna said. "Or *he's* hungry, for all I know."

The baby swung its softball-sized head around, nearly bashing Arianna in the chin.

"And in need of a change, I'd say." Arianna wrinkled her nose. "Poor baby. That guy was just hiding behind his car, waiting for someone to find the kid. What a piece of shit."

James' guilt over swearing ebbed a little. "Yeah."

He stood frozen by his own door step, unable to look away from the sight of Arianna standing there, holding the infant against her body. The *abandoned* infant. Shit... Suddenly, his life seemed like some sort of sitcom episode. Except it wasn't funny. Who the fuck did stuff like this in real life?

The kid couldn't be his. His encounters with the opposite sex had been mostly meaningless, but he wasn't stupid – he'd always taken precautions. There had to be some other answer.

The baby's wails reached a new level of noisiness, fragmenting James' half-panicked thoughts and threatening to break the sound barrier.

"Check the bag," Arianna said. "See if there's a bottle in there. And clean diapers."

Fingers numb, James crouched and fumbled with the zipper, opening the lurid vinyl sack. Inside, it was stuffed to the brim with an assortment of baby stuff. Blankets, blankets and more blankets. Tiny pieces of clothing. What looked like a rattle. "Yeah," he said, gaze finally settling on a rubber nipple protruding from between a package of wipes and a tiny, wadded-up jacket. "There's a bottle. Diapers, too."

He noticed the necessities, but his gaze was drawn to something else – something that made his gut shrivel up, cramping.

An envelope. With his name on it.

He recognized the handwriting.

There weren't many people in the world whose handwriting he would've recognized at a glance. Jed's, maybe. But the writing on the envelope wasn't his. With oversized capitals and rounded letters, it set off a chain reaction of memories, bringing the past to sudden life.

He stuffed the envelope into his pocket before Arianna could see it, then sprang to his feet.

He opened his apartment door and ushered her inside. Standing there with her and the crying baby, he set the bag down on the counter and dug the bottle out, along with a handful of diapers and a package of wipes.

"Here's everything," he said, surveying the spread of supplies that would hopefully calm the screaming baby.

"What about formula? The bottle's empty."

James buried his hands in the bag again, plunging them elbow-deep until his fingers brushed the side of a can. Pulling it out, he breathed a sigh of relief as the words 'infant formula' caught his eye. "Found it."

Arianna looked at him expectantly, and it dawned on him that she was waiting for him to make the bottle.

"I have no idea what I'm doing," he said, popping the lid off and staring at the white powder within. The can was two-thirds empty.

"There should be instructions somewhere on the label." Arianna sounded a little unsure, or maybe holding the screaming baby was just unraveling her nerves.

Either way, she was right. Hastily, James filled the bottle at the kitchen tap, then added the indicated amount of powder. After shaking the bottle, its contents resembled milk. Thank God. "Here."

"I'm not sure, but I don't think you're supposed to use tap water." Arianna took the bottle anyway.

"It's all I've got."

She nodded. "Well, it's gotta be better for the baby than starving."

She popped the bottle into the baby's mouth and was rewarded by instant silence. Silence that stretched for several minutes, until James couldn't take it anymore. "I know how this must look," he said, "but that's really not my baby."

Any second now, she'd probably hand the kid over to him and walk out the door. He wouldn't blame her – hell, he was glad she'd stuck around this long – but he didn't want her to leave with the wrong idea.

She looked up, turning those golden-green eyes on him. "How do you know?"

His heart skipped ahead, and his mouth went dry as he saw the familiar script in his mind's eye. *James*. Five letters and he knew exactly whose baby had been left on his doorstep. Maybe it shouldn't have surprised him. Maybe it *didn't* surprise him when he really thought about it. But it disappointed him, and frankly, scared him shitless. "The baby belongs to my sister."

The words left a bitter taste in his mouth. After everything he and his sister had been through, how could she? A part of him itched to tear the envelope open, to pour over whatever sorry excuse she'd stuffed inside, like anything could possibly be a good reason to do what she had. Another part of him wanted to rip it up without even reading it.

"There was a note in the bag." He didn't mention that he hadn't actually read it.

Arianna's expression changed, though he couldn't pinpoint exactly how. "Is she coming back?"

She sounded like she already knew the answer.

James' gut knotted itself a little tighter. "I don't know."

"What are you going to do?"

"I don't know."

"I guess you could call the police. Or child protective services."

James' heart slammed against his ribs, and it took all he had not to snap at Arianna. "No." His gaze was drawn to the baby, and a sense of dread he hadn't felt fully in years slipped over him. "No."

The baby had finished the bottle. Arianna held the kid against her shoulder and it burped right in her ear. She didn't seem to mind.

Grabbing one of the diapers – they were small enough to fit in the palm of James' hand – from the counter, Arianna knelt down on the floor and unraveled layers of blankets.

She'd been right about the baby needing a change. Seeing the filth the infant had been left to sit in, alone on the doorstep, filled him with sudden rage. His pulse hammered against his temples, giving him a headache, and his jaw hurt. If he'd had his sister's letter in his hands at that moment, he would've thrown it into the trash along with the dirty diaper.

"Well, you have a niece," Arianna said, securing a clean diaper and replacing the tiny pieces of clothing layer by layer. "I wonder what her name is."

James managed to grunt out something noncommittal. What the hell was he going to do?

"Does she have anything else to wear?" Arianna asked. "She spit up a little on this top."

James dug through the bag, pulling out a few articles of pint-sized clothing and handing them over. By the time the baby had been redressed, he was still standing there like an idiot, one hand buried in diapers and wadded-up blankets.

Quiet filled the apartment; not even the baby made a sound.

James felt the pressure of the silence; it sat on his shoulders like the weight of the world. Arianna was still there, still holding the baby. There was a soft look in her eyes when she looked at the kid, but now her gaze was focused on him, asking questions he didn't know the answers to.

"If you're not going to contact authorities…" Arianna reached for the bag, cradling the baby with one arm. She peered down, lowering her gaze to the supplies piled inside. "You're going to need more stuff. Babies go through everything fast – food, clothing, diapers…"

"Yeah." James just stood there, knowing she was right but unable to imagine exactly how he'd rectify the problem. What did he know about what babies needed? A shopping spree would probably turn into a total clusterfuck.

He realized he'd spoken out loud when Arianna frowned.

"It won't be that hard. Just buy the same brand of formula that came in the bag and pick diapers and clothing appropriate for her age range."

"I don't know how old she is."

"She can't be more than a month old. She's tiny and she can barely lift her own head."

Arianna lifted up the dirty bodysuit she'd set on the counter. "Baby clothes have tags saying what age range they're meant for."

She was right. The tag in question read '0-3 months'. Staring at it, he realized he was out of excuses. Unless he was going to hand the baby over to the state, he'd have to do exactly what Arianna had suggested. And there was no way he was going to involve authorities.

"I could come with you if you want help," Arianna said.

"Okay." James' lips felt numb as the word tumbled out and the reality of what he'd agreed to began to dawn on him.

What had his sister done, and what the hell could he do about it besides play along?

Nothing. And his sister would've known that. Anger simmered to the surface of his consciousness again as he contemplated her selfish actions. She had him trapped, and she knew it. Anyone who'd been through what they had would have to have a heart of stone to surrender a helpless kid to strangers' care. And though he was bitter, he wasn't that hard. He wasn't like his sister.

He had to take care of his niece, at least for the time being, until he could figure out what to do.

Feeling more like he was trapped in some bizarre dream than in real life, he walked toward the door. Arianna was still by his side, but the sexual tension had evaporated like water thrown on a hot skillet. Seducing her had quickly turned into helplessly accepting her offer of assistance. That made him feel pathetic, even though he knew he should just be grateful, for his niece's sake, that Arianna was there and willing to help.

"Let me get that," he said, stopping at the door when he realized that Arianna had crouched to place the baby back in her car seat. The thing was bulky and Arianna had to lean to one side just to pick it up.

His hand brushed hers as he grabbed the handle, relieving her of the burden. Her body heat warmed his fingers and fanned up his arm, reminding him of what he was missing out on. He'd spent months aching for her and now...

He'd be lucky if she ever came to him for so much as another tattoo after this. A baby on his doorstep – talk about a joykill.

"So how does this thing work, anyway?" he asked when they reached his car. A prickle of self-consciousness rippled down his spine as he stood there, staring at the backseat. He knew the car seat was supposed to be secured there, he just had no idea how. Standing there with the thing in one hand, it seemed like an impossible enigma. Was there a special strap or something?

"I think we're missing a piece," Arianna said. "There's supposed to be a separate base that goes in the car."

James stared toward the street, where the man who'd abandoned the baby had disappeared. "Fucking great."

"Pretty much."

"So how do I…"

"If you want, I can stay with the baby while you go shopping," Arianna said.

He turned to face her, searching her eyes for any trace of something – what, exactly, he didn't know. "You'd do that?"

"I just offered, didn't I?"

"And you're sure?"

She nodded. "It's not a big deal. I have a niece and I've babysat her a few times. It's not like I have any other plans for the evening."

He winced internally. Yeah… So much for the plans they'd had. Something deep inside him ached, but he barely noticed, he was so busy worrying about the rock and the hard place his sister had trapped him between.

"Thanks a lot," he said, reaching into his pocket and pulling out his keys. He removed one from the ring and handed it over to Arianna. "This is the key to the apartment." He'd locked the door when they'd exited it. "I'll be back as soon as I can."

She nodded and he left her with the kid, the key and the diaper bag, feeling like a dick but knowing there was little else he could've done.

He drove in a daze, pulling into the nearest Target's parking lot and taking the first space he saw. The spring air restored a little clarity to his thoughts, but all that disappeared when he reached the baby section. There was so much stuff… He gripped the handle of his cart in one hand and reached into his pocket with the other.

He called the first number on his speed dial list and breathed a sigh of relief when someone picked up on the third ring. "Hey Mina," he said. "It's James. Is Abby around?"

"She's just finishing up with a client. Do you want me to give her a message when she's done?"

"I need to talk to her. Can you ask her to call me back if she has time?" His guilt increased as he made the request, but he was desperate.

"Sure. I'll let her know."

"Thanks."

After slipping his phone back into his pocket, he began wandering up and down the aisles. An errant wheel on his cart squeaked the entire time, providing the only noise. It seemed incredibly loud as he scanned a wall of boxes stacked upon boxes, all full of diapers. He grabbed a big one that had the word 'newborn' printed in bold type on one side. Surely they would fit. After choosing a package of wipes, he rounded the corner and entered the formula aisle.

He reached for his phone, ready to call Arianna and ask what brand had been in his niece's bag. Just as he was about to dial, he realized he didn't have her number. It was in the database at Hot Ink, but he didn't have it on his cell. He considered calling Mina and asking for Arianna's number, but that would've invited questions and he wasn't ready to explain the bizarre situation he'd been thrust into. Swearing, he studied the containers lining the shelves, finally choosing one that looked like the one he'd dug out of the diaper bag.

Luckily, Abby called by the time he'd selected the formula.

"Hey," he said, "I know this is gonna sound weird and I hate to bother you while you're at work, but do you think you could tell me what kind of clothing a baby needs?" Abby had twins and was the only mother he knew well enough to ask.

A couple moments of silence ticked by, and James' gut knotted. Had he lost the connection – had she hung up on him?

"Sure. Are you buying a gift?"

"Something like that. I need to pick up the basics for a baby – a newborn, I think."

"Okay, well…" Abby talked and James listened, steering his cart through the clothing racks and trying desperately to grab everything she described.

"What about shoes?" he asked when a rack of tiny footwear caught his eye.

"Babies that young don't really need shoes. Just some warm socks or footie pajamas."

"Okay…" By the time she was done explaining, his cart was piled half full with stuff. According to Abby, babies went through several outfits a day. James tried to do the math on how much everything he'd grabbed would cost, but he'd moved too quickly. One thing was for sure – he was about to spend a shitload of money.

What was wrong with his sister – why couldn't she have sent a suitcase instead of just a little bag?

But then, if she'd given a damn about her child at all, she never would've abandoned her in the first place.

"Thanks a lot, Abby."

"It's no problem. Did you get everything you need?"

"I think so." He *hoped* so.

It wasn't until he ended the call that he saw a crib and realized he needed something for the baby to sleep in.

There was no way he'd be able to fit a crib into his car though, so instead he half-panicked until he discovered a life-saver – something called a bassinette. It was a tiny little bed and the box said it was for kids up to five months. He piled one into his cart, grabbed a few small items – pacifiers, bottles, tiny nail clippers and baby soap – and headed for the register.

Halfway there, he had to turn back to buy some of the special purified water he was apparently supposed to make bottles with. When he had a couple gallons of that in his cart, he remembered that he was missing the part of the car seat that actually allowed it to go in the car. Figuring out which base he needed to buy was a small slice of hell that involved tracking down an employee for help and calling Arianna to figure out which brand and model of seat he had.

When he finally made his way to the front of the store, the cashier gave him a weird look. Then again, maybe he was just imagining it.

"Baby on the way, huh?" she asked, scanning a pair of little pink pajamas.

James' tongue froze to the roof of his mouth. "New niece," he finally said when he worked it free.

The cashier's eyebrows skyrocketed up to her hairline. "Wow. Wish I had a brother like you when I had my kids. You must really be close to your sister." She scanned the box of diapers. "Or brother – whichever."

A bitter taste crept into James' mouth, but he didn't say anything. Silence stretched, awkward and interrupted only by the soft beeping of the register.

"$389.16," the cashier said when she'd bagged everything.

James refused to let himself wince as he dug out his wallet and ran his debit card through the scanner.

By the time he reached the parking lot, he'd stopped worrying about money. Instead, he thought of Arianna alone in his apartment with the baby. He'd been gone for a while; every time he'd been about to leave, he'd thought of something else he'd need. Now, he drove back in a hurry, on edge as he tried to think of something to say to Arianna. Something to make up for what he'd dragged her into, for the unspoken promises he hadn't fulfilled.

Even now, his entire body heated as he imagined what they'd be doing now if things had gone according to plan. He couldn't help the way he felt about her, couldn't fight the attraction that gnawed at him, even now. Which sucked, because if anyone had ever blown their chances with a woman, he had that day – spectacularly – with Arianna.

CHAPTER 3

James tried and failed to carry everything inside in one trip. In the end, he had to leave the bassinet box behind. With all his other bags in hand and the diapers under one arm, he approached his apartment door and kicked – his hands were too full to knock.

Arianna answered the door with the baby in her arms. He'd been expecting as much, but the sight still made his tongue feel heavy and his chest uncomfortably tight.

"How did shopping go?" she asked before he could say anything. Her voice was soft – probably because the baby was asleep.

"Okay. I think." He entered the apartment and set his half a dozen bags down on the living room floor, flexing his hands and willing the soreness out of them.

Baby things spilled out of his shopping bags, a pastel bounty he'd sacrificed a significant chunk of his checking account balance for. He didn't mind so much when he looked at his niece – it wasn't her fault she'd been born to a shitty mother – but his head still spun when he tried to wrap his mind around the situation.

"I've got one more thing in the car," he said, disappearing outside again and fetching the bassinette.

Arianna was still there when he got back, of course, and he still had no idea what to say. "Thanks a lot," he said, "for staying with her and everything." It was the best he could come up with, and he meant it.

Arianna nodded. "It was no problem. She slept most of the time you were gone."

Before James knew it, Arianna was approaching him. As she shifted her hold on the baby, clearly expecting James to take her, he realized he'd been wholly unprepared for this moment.

He didn't even know how to hold a baby. Doing his best to imitate the way Arianna had done it, he cradled his niece in his arms, letting her head rest in the crook of one elbow. She was lighter than he'd imagined, and warmer. He couldn't help studying her face for any signs of his sister, but it seemed too early to tell. Her rounded, chubby features could've belonged to any baby, and the swirl of dark brown hair peeking out from beneath her lopsided cap wasn't anything like his sister's long sheet of blonde strands.

She was just a baby – a person of her own. Not his sister, and not her father, whoever that was. The simple revelation struck James as he watched her eyelids flutter, so thin and pale he could see tiny blue veins branching across their delicate surfaces. In that moment, he felt profoundly sorry for her. How could anybody so tiny and helpless be so unwanted? It wasn't fair.

"Is something wrong?" Arianna's question snapped him out of his thoughts.

A thousand things that were wrong – with the situation, with the entire world – boiled to the surface of his thoughts, but the sentiments were too overwhelming to articulate.

"Someone abandoned a baby on my doorstep is all," he said, trying for a little humor.

She didn't laugh. "What are you going to do?"

He adjusted his hold, angling his arms more securely. "Take care of her for now, I guess."

She nodded slowly, saying nothing.

What did the return of her silence mean – that she was tired of him and what he'd put her through? He couldn't blame her, even if the thought did make his chest feel hollow.

"Well, I hope your sister gets her act together soon."

Now it was James' turn to nod, even though he knew there was a fat fucking chance of that. For someone who'd abandoned her newborn baby, getting her act together would be no small feat.

Arianna drifted over to the counter, picked up her purse and hitched it onto her shoulder.

James knew he had to say something. "I'm sorry things got so fucked up – that the night didn't turn out like we expected."

She paused, eyes locking with his. "Me too."

Heat flared inside him, intense but fleeting. He didn't have the balls to suggest that they pick up where they'd left off some other time. If it had been any other girl, he might have said it – might have said anything. But any other girl wouldn't have stuck around, wouldn't have sacrificed her evening to help him. Arianna was different, in a good way – that was more obvious than ever, now.

"You can call me, you know."

James' heart pounded.

"If you need any help with your niece, I mean. I'm not a baby expert, but if you don't have anyone else…"

"Thanks." He tried to rein in his disappointment. He didn't have anyone else – not really. Abby was a good friend and probably knew everything there was to know about infants, but he couldn't burden her with his problems when she had twins of her own and worked two jobs. No one else at Hot Ink had kids, and Hot Ink was his universe.

"I don't have your number. I mean, it's in the database at Hot Ink, but I don't have it on me now." He threw that out there, less embarrassed by having to ask her than he would've been by having to call in and ask Mina or Zoe for Arianna's number.

"What's yours?" She slipped her phone out of her purse. "I'll call it now and then you'll have mine in your phone."

He recited his number and even though he was expecting it, the feel of his phone vibrating in his pocket made his hand twitch. Not many people had his number, so when his phone rang, he answered it. Not this time, though. Instead he kept cradling his niece, not daring to attempt a one-handed hold.

"Thanks," he said. "I hate to say it, but you'll probably hear from me. I don't have a clue how to do any of this." At least this way, he could choose who to call when he had a question – divide his queries between Abby and Arianna so that hopefully neither one of them would get too annoyed.

Her lips quirked in the barest hint of a smile. "I wouldn't have given you my number if I minded. Feel free to call."

"Thanks." Repeating himself again, he felt like an idiot, but there was no question that she deserved his gratitude, and he wanted her to know he meant it.

"It's no problem. Really." She hitched her purse a little higher onto her shoulder, and he sensed her eagerness to leave.

Biting his tongue, he held his niece a little tighter, an automatic response to her squirming. One tiny fist hit him in the center of his chest, and he looked down at her chubby little face.

"Bet she's hungry," Arianna said.

"Already? She just ate."

"Babies eat every couple hours – sometimes more."

Shit. He'd had no idea. What would he have done if Arianna hadn't been there – unintentionally starved the kid?

A wail cut through the silence, setting his nerves on instant edge. "Looks like you're right. I'd better make a bottle." He tried to inject confidence into his voice as he panicked inwardly. The bottle-making supplies were on the counter, but his hands were full and he hadn't set up the bassinette yet. In lieu of an actual bed, he settled on lowering the baby temporarily into her car seat.

Aware of Arianna's gaze on his back, he poured some of the special water he'd bought at the store into a bottle and scanned the back of the formula container, doing a little math in his head. When he was sure he'd figured out how many scoops he'd need to add, he went ahead and dumped them in. "Am I supposed to throw this in the microwave or something?" he asked when he'd finished.

"It says on the formula container that that can be dangerous."

James frowned, scanning the container. Arianna was right. Damn it, could he be any worse at this?

"She ate the other bottle at room temperature," Arianna added, "but I bet you could warm it up a little by setting it in a bowl of warm water or something."

He considered it, but the baby was screaming and the idea of making her wait any longer was beyond daunting. Scooping her up from her car seat, he cradled her awkwardly in one arm while holding the bottle in his other hand.

Luckily, she didn't seem to have any qualms about the temperature. A sense of satisfaction rose up inside James. It was a victory, however small.

"Looks like you've got the hang of it." Arianna moved toward the door.

His heart sank, growing heavier as he prepared to watch her walk away.

"What are you going to do tomorrow when you have to go to work?" she asked, pausing at the last second, one hand on the doorknob.

His gut lurched as he contemplated the question he'd been avoiding thinking about ever since he'd embarked on his shopping spree, effectively accepting the burden his sister had passed down to him. "I don't have a damn clue."

It was woefully true. He didn't have to know anything about kids to know that he couldn't afford day care, and even if he had the cash, what were the odds he'd be able to find a babysitter by the next day?

For a few moments, Arianna didn't say anything.

Then she turned to face James. "I work from home, you know. I could watch her for you tomorrow if you want – help out while you figure out what you're going to do long-term."

It took James a few seconds to get past his disbelief. "You sure about that? You've already helped out a lot. I know it's more than I have any right to ask."

"Just give me a call tomorrow before you go in to work. I'll give you directions to my place and you can drop her off. I'll be there."

"You need a ride back to Hot Ink, right?"

Arianna shook her head. "I called a cab while you were bringing stuff in from your car. You've got your hands full here – don't worry about me."

She walked out, leaving James alone with a baby in his arms for the first time in his life.

* * * * *

Arianna breathed a sigh as she closed the door behind herself, sealing out the world in favor of the solitude of her apartment. Safely inside, she simply breathed. Her head spun with thoughts of James and the smell of baby lotion. What had she gotten herself into, exactly?

She'd promised herself she'd step out of her shell. Well, she'd definitely done that ... in a way. When she'd imagined how she'd do that, though, she hadn't been thinking of anything like what she'd just offered to do. Not even close. She'd been thinking more along the lines of getting out more – trying new things, meeting new people. Spending less time slaving away in front of her computer screen and more time being part of the world. James' invitation had seemed perfect.

Heat still smoldered deep in her core, embers of desire that warmed her from the inside out instead of dying. There was no question about it – she missed what she and James had come so close to doing. Missed it, but the pain of unfulfilled desire was overshadowed by another ache – one that radiated from the very center of her chest and into every fiber of her being.

No problem – she'd told James it was no problem for her to help him care for his niece.

She'd lied.

Deep down, she knew it was a problem. Then again, maybe that was exactly why helping him out with his niece was the perfect way to meet the challenge she'd set for herself. Taking care of the baby while he was at work would be tough, in some ways – after today, she had no doubts about that. But if doing something that set her that far outside of her comfort zone wasn't stepping out of her shell, what was?

The thought leant her a little confidence, even if the idea of babysitting the next day was still daunting. Really, she hadn't offered for her own benefit – she never would've worked up the courage to do that. No, seeing James hold his niece in his arms was what had prompted her to volunteer.

Bringing a date to a screeching halt to rescue a baby left on his doorstep, rushing to the store and bringing back a cartload of expensive supplies, planning to care for a child that wasn't even his … how many guys would do that?

He hadn't even considered calling the authorities and surrendering his niece to the state. In fact, he'd seemed pissed when she'd mentioned the possibility. He'd shocked her with his reaction, and now that shock remained, manifested in the form of an attraction even deeper than what she'd felt before.

Too bad that attraction was layered with guilt now, laced with the knowledge that he was a better person than her.

That was what it came down to, wasn't it? Before they'd discovered the surprise on his doorstep, they'd been equals – two people united by a mutual attraction, with no real plans beyond that night. The responsibility he'd been burdened with and the ease with which he'd accepted it had changed all that. There was no question: he was exceptional.

Of course, she'd known from the beginning that he was exceptionally hot, but the evening had added a whole new dimension to her perception of him – one that left her achingly aware of her own shortcomings.

* * * * *

11 Years Ago

The girls' bathroom next to the chemistry classroom was as cold as a meat locker, but sweat beaded on Arianna's forehead anyway as she slipped a hand into her purse, extracting the item she'd hidden at the very bottom of a secret pocket in the lining, beneath a stash of tampons and panty liners. She knew no one could see her inside the locked stall, but she looked around anyway, her gaze sweeping over the graffiti scribbled on the divider walls. She couldn't make out any of the words, couldn't concentrate on anything except the nearly imperceptible weight in her hand.

It'd taken all her courage to walk into a random dollar store, select the item and pay for it with a crumpled five dollar bill. She'd had to force herself to walk rather than run out of the store, deathly afraid of glimpsing a familiar face. Now, she was finally alone, hidden from view. Slowly, she unwrapped the plastic stick.

She had to force herself to concentrate long and hard enough to read the instructions that'd come with it. It took her several minutes, but the gist was simple: pee on the stick.

Actually doing it wasn't quite so easy, thanks to shaky hands. Slowly and carefully, she lifted her uniform skirt, holding onto the pregnancy test with a one-handed death grip.

She stared at the dark green plaid of her skirt, visually tracing the intersections and squares formed by the pattern, unable to bring herself to look at the test. The instructions had said to wait for a full minute before reading the results, and she couldn't bear the idea of watching them form, sweating through every second. When she was done, she sat still on the toilet, the porcelain cold against her thighs as she kept her eyes firmly shut.

After what seemed like an eternity but was probably more like thirty seconds, the door swung open, and the noise of breathless gossip and laughter invaded Arianna's sanctuary. She jumped, shoes squeaking against the floor tiles, and lost her grip on the test.

Her heart slammed painfully against her ribs during the split second it took the stick to fall, and then the plastic clattered against the tile, the sound impossibly loud. Arianna barely stifled a cry of horror as it bounced, spinning like a tiny helicopter blade, the results window a blur.

The group of girls who'd entered the bathroom had to have heard. The noise had been so loud, practically deafening to Arianna, and everything that happened in the bathroom echoed. Through the cracks between the stall door and its frame, Arianna could see a blur of legs *and bodies, tartan skirts and hair in shades of brown and gold. The girls had apparently entered to preen in front of the mirrors, though every painful beat of Arianna's heart told her that they weren't looking at their own reflections now.*

"Oh my God," one of the girls said.

Swallowing the bile that'd crept into her throat, Arianna reached down with a trembling hand and retrieved the test. Holding it tightly again, she hid the window inside her hand, not daring to look until she was alone.

The girls lingered for what seemed like an eternity, whispering things that would stick in Arianna's mind for the rest of her life. She wasn't sure what would come first: the ringing of the bell signaling the start of third period, or her own inevitable sickness. She'd been feeling nauseous most mornings for the past week, and today was no exception. She hadn't actually thrown up yet, but now it was all she could do not to puke on the floor in front of her giggling audience.

Finally, they left. Arianna released a long breath that came out half-sob, then inhaled. For a while, she simply breathed. The bell rang, but she didn't move. Finally, when she was sure everyone else had settled into class and wouldn't invade the privacy she so desperately needed, she opened her hand and looked down.

The two blue lines displayed in the test window blurred with the lines in her tartan skirt and the lines that divided the floor into thousands of tiny tiles. Arianna's head swam, and she reached out with her free hand to brace herself against the stall wall. For the rest of third period she remained hidden in the bathroom, deeply aware of the silence she'd craved and how alone she was.

* * * * *

James had made it seven hours. During that time, several bottle feedings, intermittent crying fits and half a dozen diaper changes had worn down his will. He'd definitely embarked on a crash course on infant care, whether he liked

it or not. Now, with his niece finally asleep in her bassinette –
which had taken him nearly half an hour to set up – he
wandered out to the kitchen, where he could move around
without fear of waking her.

Slowly, he slipped a hand into his pocket. The corner of
the envelope he'd stashed there earlier that day brushed his
fingertips. He pulled it out and shoved a finger under the flap,
tearing it open before he could second-guess himself.

The contents that spilled out weren't what he'd
expected. Instead of his sister's familiar scrawl, black type
spanned the papers that skittered onto the counter. As he
scanned the official-looking documents, a sinking feeling of
disappointment filled him, followed by renewed anger.

The first paper was a proof of birth letter from a
hospital in Philadelphia. It identified Crystal Layton as the
mother – no surprise there – and listed no information on the
father. That wasn't much of a surprise either, knowing
Crystal. Apparently, the baby was called Emily Sophia Layton.

He glanced toward his bedroom, where he'd left his
niece sleeping in the bassinette. Emily. According to the
hospital letter, she'd been born almost exactly a month ago,
in April.

The next several papers were stapled together and had
come from the hospital, too. Discharge papers, it looked like.
They included information on Emily – her birth weight and
blood type, stuff like that – and basic care instructions for a
newborn.

Basically, the envelope was full of things no mother
should ever give up. Of course, the same went for the baby,
so why he was surprised, he couldn't say. Maybe it was more
the fact that Crystal hadn't included a letter of her own that
had caught him off guard. That was what he'd been expecting
when he'd opened the envelope.

The fact that she hadn't bothered to write him so much as a note grated. A bitter taste filled his mouth as he flipped through the papers again. Moments later, he threw them down on the counter. He'd need them later, no doubt.

He was midway through an elaborate string of obscenities when something on the floor caught his eye – a scrap of paper.

He knelt, snatching it up. Did the torn notebook page include an excuse from Crystal? However flimsy, he wanted to read it – wanted to know how she'd tried to justify what she'd done, how she slept at night.

Sure enough, her penmanship greeted him as he unfolded the scrap of paper.

James, it read, *I need you to take care of Emily for a while. There's no one else I can turn to – you know that better than anyone. And it's because of that that I know you won't say no. Please, make sure she doesn't follow in our footsteps. Sorry, Crystal*

The note was better than nothing at all, but it was still so short that he read and reread it, as if more words might magically appear on the page. He'd expected excuses – flimsy attempts at justification that he could rage over, throw in her face if and when he ever saw her again. So why hadn't she written anything like that?

Did she realize how wrong what she'd done was? And if she did … why had she done it?

His jaw ached from being clenched so tightly. Laying down the note, he retreated to his bedroom.

Emily was still asleep, one little fist balled above the edge of the receiving blanket he'd wrapped her in.

He kicked off his jeans and sank down onto his bed, desperate for the oblivion sleep would provide, even if it wouldn't last long.

* * * * *

21 Years Ago

"I'm cold." Crystal looked up at James. Her green eyes were huge and unusually shiny. He knew that look: she'd cry if he didn't do something.

"Here." He pulled his sweatshirt over his head and handed it to her.

She stood, carefully shrugged out of her My Little Pony backpack and set it down on the stoop. After she'd wriggled her way into his sweatshirt, she put the backpack back on. She was only five, and his sweatshirt, which was a little too big for him, was huge on her. It hung, tent-like on her tiny frame, and the sleeves flapped, hiding her hands.

Sitting there on bare concrete as daylight began to fade, the October chill went right through James' t-shirt, like he wasn't wearing anything at all. He could feel it getting colder by the second, just like he could see it getting darker.

"I'm hungry," Crystal said.

"I know." He knew, and there was nothing he could do about it. Lunch at school seemed a million years ago, and his stomach was so empty it hurt. There might be food inside, or there might not – the only way to tell would be to get inside the house, and they were locked out. He'd spent five minutes knocking and yelling after the school bus had dropped them off, but no one had answered.

"It's getting dark," Crystal said. "Mom said not to be out here after dark. She said that's when the bad people come out."

"Mom's not here," James said. He wasn't sure how long he and Crystal had been sitting on the doorstep, but it seemed like hours. No matter how long he sat in the same place, the concrete felt cold as ice beneath him. "There's no way to get inside."

"She's supposed to be here," Crystal said, dragging her shoes against the concrete step so that they made a scraping sound.

"Let's play a game," James said. "I spy… Something blue."

Crystal raised an arm and flapped the end of the sweatshirt sleeve in his face. "Your sweatshirt."

He shook his head. *"Something else."*

"Hmm…"

Before she could guess again, a loud rumbling sound came from down the street.

Crystal looked at James again, and her eyes got a little bigger.

Mom said the reason dad's car was so loud was because it had a diesel engine. James could hear it from several blocks away, and the closer it got, the louder it was.

James looked back at Crystal and almost said 'go inside'. He realized how dumb that would be at the last second though, and bit his tongue.

Crystal didn't say anything, just sat there and held on tight to her backpack straps.

The car was definitely dad's. It pulled into the driveway, and James could see the rusty spots above one back wheel, and the dent above the front one. Suddenly, his stomach didn't feel empty anymore – it felt like it was tied in a million knots. He didn't feel cold, either; all the things that'd been bothering him since he'd stepped off the school bus faded away as the car door opened. None of it mattered anymore.

"What are you two doing out here? I've told you a hundred damn times if I've told you once not to be outside after dark. Get in the house." Dad looked mad, but he wasn't really yelling, so he couldn't be that upset. Yet.

"We're locked out," James said.

Dad stopped in his tracks. "What do you mean you're locked out? Where's your mother?"

"I don't know." James clenched his hands into fists. His fingernails dug into his palms, and he couldn't help squeezing until it hurt.

Dad started cussing and stopped standing still. He stumbled a little bit, but didn't fall. When he got to the steps, he grabbed James by the arm and pulled him up, so that he wasn't sitting anymore.

"Where's your damn mother?" He was yelling now. His breath smelled awful.

James held as still as he could. If he tried to get away, that would only make his father more angry. Maybe if he didn't freak out, he'd let him go. "I don't know. Nobody was here when we got home from school."

The sound of a door slamming in its frame came from next door. James turned his head, but by the time he looked, the door was shut and no one was there.

James' arm started to hurt. Dad was squeezing it. It hurt worse when he shook him and leaned in even closer. His eyes looked red, angry. "I asked you where your damn mother was, boy."

James slipped off the edge of the step. He didn't mean to, but he did. Dad didn't let go, and pain tore through James' shoulder. He hurried to stand up straight again, but dad was taller than him, and his heels didn't quite touch the ground. The pain didn't go away, just got worse every second that he stood there with just his toes against the concrete.

"Is she with Roy?" Dad shook him again. "She's with that asshole Roy again, isn't she? Fucking bitch! Fucking cheating, lying bitch!"

Dad finally let go, and James fell for real this time. The edge of the step hit his back, and he forgot all about how bad his shoulder hurt. His mouth and eyes watered, and horror filled him as he realized he was about to cry, like Crystal – like a baby. He bit his tongue to hold it back.

It didn't work.

Dad shoved a key into the lock and looked down at James. "Shut up, or I'll give you a reason to cry!"

James moved as quickly as he could, grabbing Crystal by the wrist and pulling her until they were both out of dad's way. She dropped her backpack and started to cry too, much more loudly than James; she was too little to hold most of the sound back.

Dad glared at them for a second, but it was mom he yelled and cussed at as he stomped into the house, even though she wasn't there. He didn't bother to close the door all the way behind himself, and a bar of light spilled out onto the concrete.

The sound of breaking glass came from inside the house, and James knew it didn't matter whether it was mom or him or Crystal who walked through that door: the results would be the same.

He'd been waiting for so long to go in, but now he didn't dare move. Mom's words about the 'bad people' echoed inside his head, and a prickly feeling ran up and down the back of his neck. He looked over his shoulder, but there was no one on the street. He looked back at the house and couldn't make himself go in.

CHAPTER 4

Given the fact that he'd texted her nearly an hour ago, Arianna should've been prepared to see James standing outside her apartment door.

She wasn't. As she paused at the threshold, her heart skipped a beat, then raced ahead.

"Hey," he said, eyes locking with hers as he stood cradling his niece against his chest. There was no sign of the car seat, but he carried the diaper bag slung over one shoulder. It looked fit to burst, and a tiny pink sleeve hung out one side, stuck in the zipper. The yellow daisies and lavender elephants printed on the bag contrasted with his worn jeans and charcoal grey t-shirt, which was dotted with white flecks of formula near the collar.

"Hey," she replied, steadying herself with a hand against the doorframe. "How was your first night with the baby?"

"Long." He shifted his grip on his niece, holding her a little higher on his shoulder. She was dressed in striped footie pajamas he must've picked up during his shopping trip the evening before. A matching cap hid her hair and the tips of her ears. "We both survived though, so I guess that's something."

"I never had any doubts," she said, smiling even though her insides were knotted with a strange combination of anxiety and anticipation. A part of her was looking forward to spending the day caring for a newborn. Who didn't love the smell of baby soap and the feel of silky baby hair?

Another part of her wondered just what sort of state she'd be left in when James returned after his shift and the distractions of caring for an infant ended. She'd just have to cross that bridge when she came to it.

"That makes one of us," he said. "If you'll take her, I'll head back down to the car – I picked up something on my way here."

She let him place the sleeping baby in her arms, as charmed by the way he handed her over – like she was made of glass – as she was by the weight of the child against her chest.

"Be right back." He turned and she watched him go, unable to help admiring the view. Those jeans…

The baby awoke with a grunt, opening dark blue eyes.

"Hungry, huh?" Arianna asked as the little girl began gnawing on a pudgy fist. "Let's see if you've got a bottle in here…" She knelt and dug one-handedly in the diaper bag James had put down just inside the door. Sure enough, there was a full bottle inside.

She settled down with the baby on one of her kitchen stools just as he returned, carrying a colorful baby swing.

"Realized earlier this morning that she wouldn't have anything to sleep in here." He set the little seat down on the kitchen floor. "It swings, but I didn't think to get batteries. Figure it'll still be useful, though." A plastic elephant hung above a seat fitted with nylon straps.

"I might have some batteries," she replied, thinking of the stash she kept under the kitchen sink. "I'll check as soon as she's done with her bottle."

He nodded. "Her name is Emily."

A spark of surprise flared inside her. "Did your sister get in touch with you?"

The way James frowned made her regret asking. "No. Found some papers in her bag. A birth letter, insurance card – stuff like that."

"Oh." Arianna buried an eyetooth in her inner lip, wondering if his sister had included anything else – like an explanation – but not daring to ask. "Before you leave…"

Glad for an excuse to change the subject, she tipped her head toward a roll of paper towels that sat on the counter. "You've got a little something on your shirt – just below the collar."

He blinked, crossed the kitchen and tore a towel from the roll, wetting it before scrubbing away the spit-up Emily had left on his clothing.

When he was done he raised a hand, raking it through his blond hair, which was just long enough to ripple as his fingers tore through it. The tattoos on his hands winked in and out of sight. "I hate to just dump her on you and leave, but I'm running late."

"Don't worry about it. We'll be fine. See you around eight, right?" It was slightly past noon now.

"Give or take half an hour, yeah." He advanced toward the door, looking strangely empty-handed. "Thanks again. If you think of a way I can ever pay you back, just let me know. I owe you big time."

* * * * *

"James."

"Yeah?" James turned, one hand on the half wall of his booth. There was still a faint coolness in the air, courtesy of a breeze that had followed him down the aisle as he'd hurried inside Hot Ink.

Jed stood at the end of the aisle, just outside the door to his office. James' booth was one of the very last ones, so there were hardly a few feet between them. "I need to talk to you." He tipped his head toward the open door.

James' stomach sank. Was Jed going to give him shit over almost coming in late? Usually, he was there early. Now, he was just glad his client seemed to be running five minutes late, which gave him a little time to prepare.

"It's about the wedding," Jed said when they were inside the combined office and storage area, where a desk took up one side of the room and shelves lined the other.

"Huh?"

"You know Karen and I are getting married," Jed said, his dark eyes locking with James'.

"Yeah. Everyone knows." Jed's fiancée Karen was best friends with Mina, one of Hot Ink's receptionists. As soon as their engagement had become official, the news had spread through the studio like wildfire.

Jed nodded. "Well, the wedding's coming up sooner than you might've expected. There's this wedding photographer Karen has her heart set on, but she stays booked up a year ahead of time. She had a cancellation though, and Karen knows her. She offered Karen the spot – the third weekend in June, just five weeks from now. So that's when we're holding it."

"I'm happy for you, man." He was. Everyone at Hot Ink was, especially in light of Jed's past.

"Thanks, but I'm telling you all this because I want to ask you something – will you be my best man?"

A sense of surprise rippled through James, disrupting the thoughts of Emily and Arianna that had been racing through his head ever since the evening before, clouding his ability to focus on anything else. "You want me to be your best man?"

"Yeah. You're not surprised, are you?"

He was, though he didn't say it. He and Jed had been close for years; it wasn't weird, when he thought about it. He just wasn't used to thinking about anyone holding him in such high regard – old habits died hard.

"You'll do it, right?" Jed leaned against the desk, arms crossed.

"You know I will." There wasn't much Jed could've asked him for that he would've said no to, and being a part of his wedding wasn't even close to being on that list.

"Great. Weeks away is last minute when it comes to planning a wedding, according to Karen."

"I wouldn't know."

"Don't worry – you couldn't stop her from handling all the details if you tried. She'll probably want you to get fitted for a tux sometime soon though."

James nodded. "That's not a problem."

"Good—"

A soft knock sounded, and the door swung inward.

"Hey James," Zoe said, poking her head inside. "Just thought you'd want to know your client's here."

"Thanks." He nodded to Jed and exited the office, striding out into the waiting area to greet the guy who he'd last seen for a consult a month and a half ago.

"You ready for this tattoo?" he asked, mentally reviewing the design he'd finished a couple weeks ago. When he was done, it'd be something his client could be proud of for the rest of his life. Still, he couldn't shake the feeling that it'd pale in comparison to the last tattoo he'd done – Arianna's sugar skull design.

Then again, maybe that thought had as much to do with the incredible body he'd laid that ink into as it did with the design itself. It wasn't like he'd been able to stop thinking of Arianna and what they'd missed out on, even with Emily to distract him. No, he had a serious case of blue balls and it wasn't like he'd had any time to do anything about it the night before. As a result, he still ached for Arianna, and the thought of her colored everything he did. Stopping by her apartment that night for purely practical reasons was going to be a sweet sort of hell.

* * * * *

A shiver zipped down Arianna's spine as water coursed down her arm, sweeping over her fresh tattoo and washing soap bubbles from her skin. The water was colder than she'd expected.

Adjusting the bathroom faucet, she held a washcloth under the now lukewarm flow and squeezed it over her arm, repeating the process. Gently, she used her fingertips to massage the last traces of mild soap from her skin, not daring to use anything rougher.

A knock came at the door, and she dropped the washcloth. It landed on top of one of her feet with a *splat*. Bending to pick it up, she crossed the small bathroom and took a dry one from the closet, then patted her arm dry.

Freshly washed, the sugar skull stared up at her, an errant bead of water shining from the corner of one eye socket, tear-like. The healing process had just begun, but it was obvious that as long as she took good care of it, the tattoo would be gorgeous. The thought was satisfying but quickly relegated to the backburner of her mind, overshadowed by nervous anticipation as she made her way through the living room, toward the door.

"Coming," she called softly – probably too softly for James to even hear. Emily was sleeping in her swing, beside the couch, and she didn't want to wake her.

Sure enough, it was James who'd knocked. He looked much like he had that morning, minus the white stain on his shirt. There were dark circles under his eyes, but she hardly noticed them, the grey-green of his irises was so distracting. "You're a little early."

"My last client was like you – didn't want to stop for any breaks. Saved me some time. Figured you'd be glad."

She *was* glad to see him, but not because watching his niece had been bad. Actually, she'd enjoyed it – mostly. Now, she was a little afraid of how empty her apartment might seem when James and Emily were gone. Spending the day tending to a newborn had been a dramatic change from her usual days passed in silence in front of her computer screen – a change that had emphasized just how lonely her days typically were.

"Emily was no trouble." She tipped her head toward the swing. "She's fast asleep now – ate a whole bottle about half an hour ago."

James nodded and strode across the room, picking up the diaper bag by the strap and hefting it onto his shoulder.

Arianna's gaze drifted back to the purple shadows under his eyes. "I'm sure she'll sleep for a little while longer, if you'd like a cup of coffee. You look really tired."

He hesitated for a moment, then nodded. "Coffee would be great."

She set to work making him some. She had a single cup brewer, so it only took a minute. When she was done, she made one for herself, too, and they settled at the kitchen table. "Cream and sugar?"

He shrugged. "If you don't mind — anything to stay awake at this point."

Moments later, as she watched him raise the steaming cup to his lips, a frisson zipped down her spine. It wasn't unlike the one that had affected her minutes ago, as cold water had coursed down her arm. This time though, it had nothing to do with her new tattoo and everything to do with the man who'd given it to her. "Was last night rough?"

James met her eyes over the rim of his coffee cup, and his free hand twitched against the table, like he wanted to be doing something else with it. Raking it through his hair, maybe. "Last night wasn't that bad, to be honest. It was today that was rough. All day, I couldn't stop thinking about Emily — wondering what the hell I was going to do. You saved my ass today, but there's still tomorrow. And the next day…"

He took a long drink of his coffee, steam rising and curling in front of his face. Hopefully, he wasn't burning his tongue.

Arianna took a more modest sip of her own drink, hiding the reflexive frown that leapt to her lips as she studied the lines worry had etched across his forehead. "You're not counting on your sister showing up anytime soon, huh?"

He shrugged, shoulders jerking in a rigid motion. "How can I count on anyone who'd abandon their own kid? She left a note in the bag, but it didn't say much."

"And you're going to do what she was counting on — take care of Emily for however long she's gone?"

He didn't shrug this time. Instead, he lowered his cup and raked his hand through his hair, pausing afterward to touch the bridge of his nose. He didn't seem to notice he'd done it, but it drew Arianna's attention to the bump there. He must've broken it at some point.

"Yeah," he finally said. "It's not like she has anywhere else to go. I can't just abandon her — no kid deserves that."

His eyes seemed to turn a darker shade of grey-green, as if cast in shadow.

She didn't ask whether James had any other family members who might help take care of Emily. Obviously, he didn't – why else would he have turned to her, someone he barely knew? Clearly, he was on his own. "Do you have work tomorrow?"

He nodded.

"I'll watch her again for you. Just drop her off—"

He shook his head. "I already feel bad for leaving her with you today. You don't have to keep helping me – this isn't your problem."

Maybe it shouldn't have been, but she'd been there when he'd discovered the baby on his doorstep and now she couldn't help but feel like she'd be abandoning him, somehow, if she didn't lend a hand. Plus, she liked him – maybe more than she had a right to. Seeing the dark circles beneath his eyes and the lines across his forehead made her ache to ease what was bothering him.

"I want to help. Really."

He shook his head again. "You have a job, too. I know you can't be getting any work done with Emily around. Leaving her with you – someone I barely know – so that I can go off and do my own thing… Maybe I'm not much better than my sister."

His words sent a ripple of shock through Arianna. "Don't say that – it's ridiculous. And actually, I got quite a bit done today while she was napping. I had a full night's sleep last night, so it's not like I needed to rest while she was sleeping, and newborns sleep a lot. I mean it; you can keep dropping her off here whenever you have work, until you figure something else out."

He met her eyes again, and she got the feeling that he was searching for … something. His expression was a little guarded, but his eyes were clear, windows wide open to project his uncertainty. "I don't want to take advantage of you."

"If it gets to be too much, I'll let you know." She wouldn't back out after giving her word, but he looked like he needed reassurance. "I actually enjoyed today."

A cry came from the living room, and James turned in his seat.

Arianna craned her neck to look at Emily. "Looks like she spit out her pacifier." She leapt up before James could do the same and crossed the room, picking up the pacifier from where it had landed in Emily's lap and placing it back in her mouth.

She settled back down immediately, slipping back into silent sleep.

When Arianna returned to the kitchen, James was standing. His eyes traveled over her body, lingering on her arm and then snapping up to meet her gaze. "How's your new tattoo?"

She stopped beside him, glancing down at his coffee cup and seeing that it was empty already. "I think it looks great, don't you? It's just starting to heal."

He raised a hand, touching her upper arm lightly, just above one of the marigolds that framed the skull. "Yeah. It looks great. Sugar skulls are a Mexican thing, right?"

"Yes. I've always liked them... I guess some people might think they're a little creepy, but I think they're gorgeous. Plus, one of my grandmothers is Mexican, and I thought it'd be nice to have a tattoo that reflected that part of my heritage."

"I don't think it's creepy at all. It's beautiful, like you said, and if it means something to you, so much the better. Yours is the first one I've tattooed."

"Yeah, well, you have to pierce anyone who walks into Hot Ink anywhere they want, so you probably have a different concept of 'creepy' than most." She smiled to let him know she was teasing, remembering the conversation they'd had when he'd tattooed her last. It was nice to have an excuse to smile, because with him touching her, it was impossible not to.

An answering smile flickered across his face. "Hey, somebody's gotta do it."

"What inspired you to pierce people, anyway? None of the other artists at Hot Ink do it."

He looked thoughtful for a moment, then shrugged. "Like you said, none of the other artists at Hot Ink do it. It seemed logical to learn and to offer the service. Plus…" His smile flashed back into place, then broke into a full-fledged grin. "There's always the chance that I'll get to pierce somebody like you *anywhere you want*."

It was obvious he was only teasing, but the heat of a blush spread across her face anyway. "I guess piercing other guys' hairy nipples is the other side of the coin," she replied, doing her best to keep her voice steady.

He nodded, looking grave. "Yeah, it is."

"So, do you think you'll ever get any piercings? I mean, tattoo artists always have tattoos, right? And you have a ton of those." Her gaze flickered to his arms, where ink extended all the way to his hands. A trail of stars stood out bold and dark on one arm, drawing her eye, but what she liked best were the mandala designs decorating his hands, sprawling dark and intricate to the edges of his knuckles. "But you pierce people, and you don't have any piercings."

"What makes you think I don't have any?"

His reply caught her off guard. As an avalanche of possibilities spilled through her mind, she searched his eyes. A teasing light shone there – did that mean he wasn't serious?

"Well, I don't see any piercings," she said bravely, willing away the heat that threatened to creep to the surface of her skin.

"You can't see all my tattoos, either, but you don't think these are the only ones I have, do you?" He raised his arms.

"Well, when you put it that way…" Something caught Arianna's attention, just barely visible in the corner of her eye. Grateful for the excuse to look away, she turned and picked up the baby bottle from the kitchen counter. She'd almost forgotten about it. Now, she turned on the hot water and washed it, eyes fixed on the sink's steel interior.

Maybe he was only teasing, but regardless, she couldn't stop thinking about where his piercing might be if he did have one. Somewhere hidden by his clothing, obviously. Maybe her imagination was stunted, but she could only think of a couple places where that might be.

She'd spent enough time staring at him to know that his chest was smooth beneath his shirt, a flat surface without any bumps that might betray piercings there. No nipple rings, then. Which left…

Heat struck her, but not the heat of embarrassment this time. Instead, it was lust. Whether he was pierced or not, she'd come incredibly close to finding out. Now she'd probably never know. The thought weighed in her chest like a stone, dragging down her spirits.

When she turned around, drying the bottle with a paper towel, she nearly bumped into him.

His nearness shocked her into silence. When had he come so close? She could practically feel his body heat, could smell the soap on his skin and clothing. And she'd never had such a good look at his eyes, even when he'd been tattooing her. That realization heightened her surprise, and she couldn't look or move away. Not that she wanted to.

She sensed his intent just like she sensed his heat, his scent. In the space of a few short seconds, the spark that had flared between them the day before was rekindled. Maybe it had been the conversation, the teasing – for the first time since James' life had taken a turn for the unexpected, they'd spoken about something other than his new responsibility and the issues it raised. Whatever the reason, they were as close as two people could be without touching.

And then he did touch her, fingers brushing her arm, skimming down all the way to her wrist and settling on her hip.

CHAPTER 5

He pressed his lips against hers before she could react, sealing their first kiss with heat and just enough pressure to make her tingle all over. The unabashedly intimate contact was a welcome relief after what she'd endured for so many hours during their tattoo sessions: his hands on her body, fingertips veiled by the gloves he wore when he worked. The desire she'd felt for him then intensified to the point that it almost hurt now, and she melted against him, body pressing against the hard plane of his chest, her hip touching his.

He was even harder there – his cock pressed against her lower belly, unmissable. An extra burst of heat flared inside her as she remembered the way he'd teased her. Or maybe he hadn't really been teasing. Between her jeans and his, she couldn't tell if it was pierced. The thought ignited a potent sense of curiosity, and just thinking about seeing him naked sent tremors racing through her limbs, daring her to do something to make it happen.

Instead, she savored his kiss. He tasted like coffee, and his lips were hot from the mug, his tongue faintly sweet as he swept it between her lips, just barely touching hers.

The moment she responded, allowing their tongues to slip together, Emily cried.

It started out as a whine and quickly escalated into a wail – one that made it clear she didn't appreciate being ignored.

It was as if a brick wall had been slammed between Arianna and James. They both turned toward Emily's swing at the same time, bumping into each other and nearly tripping.

Arianna gripped James' arm out of reflex in order to avoid falling on her face.

He sucked in a breath and reached out to steady her before rushing forward again, all without meeting her eyes.

As she stood tingling in the wake of his touch, he beat her to Emily. Scooping the baby up into his arms was all it took to reduce her crying to halfhearted sniffles.

For a few seconds, Arianna just stared. When she'd first met James, during their initial tattoo consultation nearly a year ago, she'd had a hard time looking away and an even harder time keeping him off her mind after she'd left. What she'd felt then was nothing compared to what she felt now.

The contrast of the tiny newborn and James' large, hard frame was overwhelming and undeniably appealing to look at. Though he was obviously new to caring for a child, he handled his niece delicately. Why couldn't all men be like him?

The thought came out of nowhere, hitting Arianna hard and shining light on a dark place she tried not to think about. Biting down on her inner lip, she turned to face the counter and picked up the bottle she'd recently washed. "You'd better feed her before you go, or she'll probably get fussy in the car."

She made the bottle while he held Emily, then handed it over to him, her fingertips shaking slightly when she was left empty handed.

Fifteen minutes passed by in silence, then the bottle was half empty and Emily was asleep in James' arms.

"Thanks again," he said as he strapped her into her car seat. "Like I said, I owe you."

"I'll see you tomorrow," she replied, another pang of unwanted emotion sailing through her chest.

He met her eyes. "You sure?"

"I told you I was. I'm not backing out now."

He nodded. "Free tattoos for life. And piercings." The barest hint of a smile played around the corners of his mouth, and his gaze roved briefly over her body before he met her eyes again. "And if you think of anything else you might want…"

Her body temperature seemed to rise by a few degrees, leaving her feeling half-fevered. She wasn't sure if she loved or hated that she couldn't tell for sure when he was teasing and when he wasn't.

Before she could decide what he was serious about and what he wasn't, he was gone.

* * * * *

James threw his phone down hard on the bed.

It bounced off a pillow and onto the mattress, unscathed, its screen still illuminated. According to it, his most recent call had lasted barely two minutes. He'd spent most of it on hold, and that was all it had taken to discover that the hospital in Philly where Emily had been born absolutely would not give him any information on Crystal. Not an address or a phone number – not even confirmation that she'd been a patient there just a month ago.

It wasn't surprising – there were privacy laws and all that – but it was disappointing. He'd been wracking his mind for two days now, trying to figure out how to get in touch with Crystal, and calling the hospital where she'd given birth had been the best idea he'd been able to come up with.

Now, he had nothing, no way to get in touch with her.

Crystal might as well have never existed, except she'd left something of herself behind – her own flesh and blood.

He had no idea why she'd done it or where she'd gone, and he might never see or hear from her again.

In her bassinette beside the bed, Emily stirred, one little fist emerging from the blanket he'd wrapped her in and flailing. She opened her eyes, staring at him with dark blue irises that had yet to reveal their true color.

Bending at the waist, he scooped her out of her bed and held her. Contemplating what he'd do if Crystal never showed up, he felt more alone than he ever had when he'd had his apartment and his life all to himself.

* * * * *

11 Years Ago

Arianna had sweated more during the past 24 hours than she had in her entire life. At the moment, her perspiration was probably ruining the make-up she'd so carefully applied, eager to look better than she felt as she broached the most important conversation of her life.

"What's your problem?" Cody asked, his breath hot against her neck.

Arianna's breath caught in her throat, and although this was an obvious opportunity to confess, she stalled. "What do you mean?"

"You're acting so lame today. It's like you don't want to do anything."

Arianna looked up at Cody, and for once she didn't wonder how much time she'd be able to talk her parents into letting her spend with him that week. Instead, she thought about the secret hidden away in the bottom of her purse – the positive pregnancy test she'd been smuggling around all day, feeling more like a drug lord than a Catholic highschool sophomore.

"I don't feel very good," she admitted.

"Well why'd you come over then? I thought you wanted to have fun." He flopped back onto his bed, breathing a sigh of disappointment. A movie they weren't watching blared in the background, the only noise in his bedroom for several long moments.

"I wanted to talk to you," she said. After school, she'd had to beg her parents to let her go to Cody's place. She'd only gotten away with it because she'd promised he'd help her with her algebra homework. Presumably, they'd believed he'd be some help because he was a senior and earning B minuses in calculus.

"About what?" He remained on his bed, staring up at the ceiling.

When Arianna had imagined this conversation, it had involved eye contact. Biting back a sigh of frustration, she stood up and moved so that he could see her, sinking down onto the edge of the bed beside him just in time to hide the fact that her legs were wobbling.

"Is it about that party Brandon's having on Friday? 'Cuz I don't see why your parents won't let you go, but I'm not going to miss out just because they're being—"

"No." A sick feeling struck Arianna, but for once, she couldn't chalk it up to the nausea typical of pregnancy. "Cody..." She studied his face, searching for the look she'd seen there when he'd made her heart skip beats, when he'd listened to her talk about her frustrations with her parents and sister and agreed that they were unfair. When he'd kissed her, making her forget about it all.

Right now, she couldn't see the boy who'd made her feel so special, but maybe that was just because she was so stressed out. As tongue-tied as she was now that it came down to it, she longed to share her burden with him, to feel his arms around her and hear him tell her that it would be okay, just like he'd done a few weeks ago when she'd gotten into a big fight with her mom. The memory of his reassurances loosened her tongue a little, fortifying her resolve.

"I have to tell you something," she said, gripping her purse. "I..."

He met her eyes, and her heart picked up pace. A million seconds seemed to slip by in silence before she finally said it: "I'm pregnant".

It didn't take nearly so long for him to answer. "No you're not."

She had to turn his simple reply over in her mind several times, and even then, it didn't make sense. "Yes I am."

He looked at her like she'd just told him she'd been abducted by aliens. "Are you joking?"

His disbelief sliced right through her, cutting to the quick. "No. Why would you think I'd joke about something like this?"

He shook his head and looked away, swearing under his breath. "So are you saying it's mine?"

"Yes." Her voice came out quiet and strained, though a part of her felt like screaming. "Who else's would it be?"

He shrugged, and her heart caved in. "I can't believe you think I'd cheat on you! You know you're the only person I've ever been with."

Even more disturbing than his insinuation was the fact that he didn't seem at all bothered by it. Arianna's head spun, and she gripped her own arms, willing a fresh bout of nausea to go away. It didn't, and she had to hurry down the hall to his bathroom. When she emerged, he was waiting.

The horrible tension spiraling in her middle eased a little as she waited for him to snap out of whatever was wrong with him, to finally reach out and touch her.

"At least you realized early on," he said.

"What do you mean?"

He stared pointedly at her belly. "I mean, you're not even fat yet. It should be easy to get rid of it."

A deeper sense of sickness gripped her then, and she knew no amount of vomiting would dispel it. The world blurred around her, though Cody's words rang in perfect clarity, a death sentence not to their unborn child, but to everything she'd believed and clung to – everything she'd treasured.

"I can't believe you," she said. "What's – what's wrong with you?"

"Well it's not like I'm going to be stuck with some baby," he said, as if that explained everything.

"I…" The oasis of comfort she'd longed for all day had turned out to be nothing more than a mirage, and the discovery threatened to bring her to her knees. She searched for the right words to convey a disappointment deeper than she'd known was possible, a disillusionment so harsh it seemed to have stripped the very skin from her body, leaving her one giant, walking wound.

Her mind was a dry well, the perfect English and passable Spanish she spoke both utterly insufficient. There were no words to describe what she felt as she stared at the stranger who'd just said the unthinkable. She couldn't say whether her heart was actually broken, because all she could feel in its place was a vast, aching emptiness that swallowed her as she stood there, more alone than she'd ever been.

* * * * *

Standing at Arianna's apartment door with a baby cradled in one arm and a bouquet in the other, James felt so nervous he might as well have been 18 instead of 28. The flowers had been an impulse buy, something he'd picked up at the grocery store on his way over, where he'd stopped to make an emergency baby wipes purchase.

It was amazing how quickly the kid went through those things. Over the past week, he'd used an entire economy sized package. Baby supplies had definitely put a dent in his budget already, and yet, he'd picked up the flowers without even glancing at the price tag.

Maybe it was the fact that the red carnations included in the bundle of blossoms reminded him a little of the marigolds he'd inked into Arianna's skin just a week ago. Or maybe it was just that anything beautiful had a way of turning his thoughts to her. Either way, the flowers had caught his eye and he hadn't been able to resist buying them for her.

Now, he second-guessed the wisdom of that whim. He owed her so much... A bouquet from the grocery store's little floral section next to the pharmacy wasn't even a drop in the bucket. What if it seemed like an insult instead of a show of his appreciation?

And then there was the fact that his appreciation was only part of the reason why he'd bought the flowers. Not so deep down, he wished he was dating her – ached to romance her, somehow. The warm weight in the crook of his arm reminded him of exactly why that wasn't going to happen. In his mind, he relived his and Arianna's one and only kiss anyway.

God, it'd felt good to press his lips to hers, to taste her. He'd have done it again if there hadn't been the distraction of Emily, plus the weight of all that he owed Arianna – roughly equivalent to the weight of the world – between them. He hadn't been able to resist doing it at least once, but she'd babysat five days for him since then, and every day deepened his debt to her. He didn't dare take advantage of her in a whole new way when she was already doing so much for him. God knew she was probably getting sick of seeing his face as it was.

Gripping the bouquet, he knocked with the flowers in hand. Shaken, the blossoms released a subtle perfume. The scent reminded him of how her hair had smelled when he'd kissed her.

By the time she opened the door, his mouth was watering at the remembered taste of her. Maybe it was weird to feel that way when he was in charge of Emily, but taking care of her was a 24/7 job, and he was only human. He couldn't just shut off what made him tick because of his new responsibilities, and he couldn't shut off his feelings for Arianna, either.

"Hey." She stood in the doorway, looking characteristically gorgeous in jeans and a plain white cami that let the colorful ink on her arms take center stage, drawing the eye.

"Hey." One would've thought he'd gotten used to seeing her almost every day, but that wasn't the case. Standing there, he stared.

"What are those?"

He looked down, following her gaze.

The flowers. Shit. Had he really forgotten about them in the two seconds it'd taken her to open the door?

Maybe more blood had migrated away from his brain than he'd realized. To distract her from that fact, he thrust the bouquet at her. "They're for you." He started to say some bullshit about how they were meant to show his thanks for all the help she'd given him, but his tongue froze to the roof of his mouth.

He just couldn't bring himself to say it, because as she accepted the bouquet, her fingers brushed his and that was all it took to make him realize that buying the flowers had had everything to do with the fact that he longed to seduce her, no matter how unconducive the circumstances.

Logically, he knew he was off to a shitty start, as far as romance went. He'd dug himself into a deep hole, and clawing his way out so that he could stand on equal footing with her would be one hell of a job. Maybe somehow, though, if he—

"They're beautiful." Arianna smiled, and it reached all the way to her eyes, causing them to shine and crinkle a little at the corners. "Thanks."

"I, uh—" Her smile shot his hopes way up, filling his head with improbable scenarios. His tongue remained uncooperative – not that he could think of anything to say that didn't sound fucking idiotic, anyway.

Emily squirmed in his arms, and he readjusted her against his chest.

"Are you going to come in or what? That bag looks heavy."

In truth, his mind barely registered the weight of the diaper bag he'd slung over one shoulder.

"Is today some sort of special occasion?" Arianna asked as she pulled the apartment door shut.

"No," James said, casting a guilty glance toward the flowers. "I just saw the flowers and thought of you."

Arianna tipped her head toward Emily. "But Emily's all dressed up. Between that and the flowers, I thought maybe there was something going on that I didn't know about."

James glanced down at Emily, whose tiny legs protruded from beneath the flounces of a layered skirt. Glitter winked from the edges of the tulle, matching the little shoes that'd been made to go with the dress. "This? Got it at the store while I was on a formula run. It was on clearance." He shrugged, his uneasiness increasing.

How could he explain the thoughts that'd gone through his head when he'd seen the dress? That he hated the thought of an unwanted child, that he wanted Emily to have all the things that normal, cherished children had... That buying the outfit and dressing her up like a tiny doll had eased a little of the guilt he felt over being pissed at Crystal for dumping Emily on him.

"When we were little, my mom used to put my sister and me in dresses like that every Sunday for church."

"Guess it's a little weird to put her in one for no reason," he admitted. Dressing Emily in the elaborate outfit had taken at least 10 minutes. "There are pajamas in the diaper bag if you want her to wear something else."

Arianna shook her head. "No way – the dress is adorable. I'm just afraid I'll spill formula on it or she'll spit up and it'll get stained."

"Don't worry about it. I didn't spend much on it."

"Okay, if you're sure."

James put Emily down in her swing, and miracle of miracles, she stayed asleep. Usually, she slept soundly during the ride to Arianna's, then was woken up by the commotion of being unloaded from the car and carried up the steps. Rising, James found himself alone with Arianna – or as close to being alone with her as he was likely to ever get again, anyway.

She still clutched the bouquet he'd given her. "I'd better get these in some water."

He watched her as she turned and bent to rummage in a cupboard, eventually pulling out an empty pitcher and filling it halfway at the tap. In a split second, he went from thinking about baby clothes to noticing how well Arianna filled out her jeans. He was officially hopeless – he'd never be able to stop wanting her.

She set the flowers in the middle of the table, and they looked good there. "Coffee?" she asked. "You have perma-circles under your eyes."

He glanced at the clock hanging on the kitchen wall. "If you don't mind."

He'd gotten into the habit of leaving 20 minutes early – something he'd learned was necessary when you were traveling with a baby. Emily had a tendency to either spit up or need a diaper change two seconds after he walked out the door. Today, she'd done neither, so he had a little time to spare.

"I'm all out of half and half," she said. "There's sugar, though."

"Black's fine." It wasn't like he'd taste the coffee, anyway. Arianna dominated his thoughts, and his senses were devoted to the memory of their single kiss, to the feel and taste of her.

She set the coffee in front of him, then settled down in the chair beside his. "Have you been getting *any* sleep?"

He shrugged. "I think so. Sometimes the only way I can be sure if I fell asleep between feedings or not is if I can remember a weird dream I had – something too bizarre to be real."

She nodded. "You know, if you can't get caught up, you could leave her here for a night. It'd give you a chance to get some rest—"

He was wrong – he did taste the coffee. It was bitter, in sharp contrast to Arianna's overwhelming sweetness. "No way. You've been watching her for me every day. I'm not leaving her here overnight."

Arianna frowned. "You just look so exhausted—"

"No. Thanks, but no."

Her frown didn't waver. She looked at him, and he got the distinct feeling she was sizing him up, trying to see inside his head.

"You know what I can't figure out?" The words tumbled from his mouth. "Why you're so nice to me. Why do you care how much sleep I'm getting?"

If she'd wanted to know what he was thinking, she'd gotten it.

For a second, it seemed like he'd surprised her into silence.

"I like you," she said eventually. "Is that a good enough reason?"

"Seems like you'd have to like me an awful lot to put yourself through all this." Sarcasm leant his voice an edge. He wasn't special enough to warrant a beautiful woman like

Arianna bending over backwards to basically work as an unpaid nanny for him. Who was?

"I do."

He took a long drink of his coffee, singeing the tip of his tongue. "It's a little hard to believe."

"I know she's your niece, not mine, but I was there when you found her. We were together and it just would've seemed … wrong to walk away and let you deal with it all on your own. You weren't expecting it any more than I was, even if she is your sister's kid."

"It wouldn't have been wrong. No one else would've stuck around. Hell, my sister didn't even stick around for her own kid. Or the father, whoever he is. I think you have a hyperactive conscience." If only that'd been the case with his sister. The thought almost made him laugh.

Arianna shrugged. "It's too late now. I like you too much to leave you all on your own at this point."

He almost smiled. Her words were bittersweet – exactly what part of him wanted to hear, while another part of him wondered why and how that could even be true. Yeah, there was physical chemistry between them. So much of it that if their one and only date had gone as planned, he had no doubt it would've been the hottest night of his life. But there hadn't been much time for anything like that since then.

"I like you too," he said, "though after all you've done for me and Emily, I'd be a pretty big piece of shit if I didn't."

Her lush mouth quirked down into a frown so fleeting he wondered if he'd imagined it.

"Well," she said, "I hope my babysitting services aren't the only reason you like me." Her voice was light, teasing, but her eyes weren't.

As unbelievable as it was, she actually looked wary. She pressed her hands against the table as if bracing herself for something, and her eyes were intense as they searched his, presumably ready to read between the lines of whatever answer he gave.

She was waiting to be judged. He recognized the feeling because he'd experienced it himself so many times before.

He'd hated that feeling, almost as much as he hated seeing it reflected in her eyes now.

He stood so fast his chair almost toppled over. Barely avoiding spilling his coffee, he leaned over, slipping a hand behind her head and letting his fingers get tangled in her hair. "It's not the only reason. Not even close."

He kissed her without caring whether he was just using the situation as an excuse. He'd worry about that later – for now, all he could think about was making sure she knew exactly how much he liked her.

Maybe he had coffee breath, or maybe he'd just startled her. Either way, she froze, unmoving as he pressed his lips to hers.

Her reaction didn't last long. After a couple seconds of his mouth against hers and his fingers wrapped in her hair, she gave in.

Relief coursed through him, as potent as his lust. Their tongues tangled together, and a soft noise was caught somewhere between her mouth and his – a moan.

The sound bolstered his confidence in a way nothing else could have. Burying his hand deeper in her hair, he let his fingertips cradle the curve of her skull, causing an answering prickling sensation to rush over his, making his hair stand on end.

His cock did something similar, or at least would've if it hadn't been for his jeans. Their restraint caused an ache in his groin. It mirrored the one in his balls – a pain he'd been living with for the past week. It only grew worse as he laid his free hand on her body, first on her hip and then skimming upward, over the curve of her side.

When he cupped her breast, she leaned into him, filling his palm with soft flesh that was easily felt beneath the thin cover of her cami. Vivid fantasies sprang to life in his mind. It'd be so easy to slip those straps down, exposing skin he'd never seen, not even while tattooing her.

Fantasy blurred with reality as she rose, crushing her body against his before he could lose his grip on her or break their kiss. If the full length of her torso pressed against the full length of his cock wasn't an invitation, he didn't know what was.

CHAPTER 6

His fingertips tingled as he ran them over the slope of her breast. Did she feel the same sensation where he touched her, beneath her clothing?

The way she kissed him back made it seem like she did, and though a breathless silence had descended on them both, the sound of her moan echoed in his mind, driving him on. In a matter of moments, he'd caught one of her top's narrow straps between his fingers and was peeling it down over the slope of her shoulder, just like he'd imagined.

Her bra was strapless. It hugged her ribcage, supporting breasts he sometimes found himself dreaming about, half in and half out of sleep. Those fantasies had a way of evaporating as he rolled out of bed, retreating to the back of his mind and lingering there, saturating his subconscious with a relentless craving for Arianna. Now, he was living the dream, his fingertips drifting over the double-swell of her cleavage, then dipping into a bra cup and teasing the hard peak he found there.

She arched against him, her back bowing as their mouths were pressed more tightly together. His lower lip ached beneath the pressure, and then she bit it lightly.

Holy fuck. A tremor raced through the center of his being, sending a jolt of urgency straight to his cock. He wanted her so bad that in his mind's eye, he could see himself lifting her onto the table and tearing her jeans off, bringing his waking-dream to completion by burying himself inside her. He contemplated the logistics automatically, factoring in her apparent eagerness – he could have her legs wrapped around his hips in less than a minute.

There was only one problem: he didn't have a condom.

He had a box back at his apartment, but it wasn't like he'd expected this, and he didn't carry a stash around in the diaper bag just in case. He hadn't dared to indulge that kind of optimism.

As quiet and reserved as she was, Arianna didn't seem like she'd have a contingency supply of contraceptives on hand, either. Then again, she sure as hell didn't seem reserved at the moment. There was definitely a side to her he hadn't seen until now.

Maybe she was on the pill. And if that was the case, maybe she'd be all right with foregoing a condom. He knew he was clean, and as long as she was too…

She gave another one of those moans when he undid her jeans' button and pulled down the zipper.

He reveled in her wordless approval … until she gripped his wrist, hard.

They both stopped cold, lips slipping apart.

Her pupils were dilated, her cheeks flushed and lips swollen. As she met his eyes, all he could do was stare. Just looking at her like that – what he'd done to her – was almost as good as having his tongue wrapped up with hers.

Her nails bit into his skin as she clung to his arm, her lush lips turning down at the corners. "I'm not on the pill or anything like that."

That brought his hopes down. A little, anyway. "Don't worry about it."

He slipped his fingers into the open V of her jeans' zipper. Her panties were soft against his skin, and her body heat radiated through them. Soon he'd know if she was wet beneath – if she wanted this as badly as he wanted to do it to her.

"What do you mean, 'don't worry about it'?" Her words came out strained. She'd let go of his wrist, but her voice was hard and cold as steel. Talk about a 180…

He met her gaze, and the look she was giving him froze him, his hand still inside her jeans, his fingertips the barest fraction of an inch away from her clit.

"Fuck. Not like that." Realization dawned on him, sudden and harsh. "I didn't mean…"

He wanted to be inside her, wanted to feel her pussy wrapped so tightly around his dick he didn't know where he ended and she began. But he'd never let that happen without making sure they were safe, first. He told her that, frozen with his hands on her body, his hopes stuck in his throat, along with his heart.

Her expression softened a little, giving way to a look that was more wary than accusing. "Then what are you doing?"

"Let me show you."

She let him shimmy her jeans off and lift her onto the table, which proved sturdy enough to hold her weight. Her body wasn't as pliant beneath his hands as it had been only minutes ago, but he figured he had his own fuck-up to thank for that. He'd just have to ease her back into that state, make her feel so good she forgot all about the dumbass way he'd worded things.

Beneath the hem of her cami, the edge of the tattoo on her left hip peeked out at him. He'd done that one for her – it was an abstract design, all swirls and vivid colors that stood out bright and bold against her golden-olive skin. He'd been intrigued when she'd requested him to design it for her, and he'd drawn it directly onto her skin, allowing his marker and then his tattoo machine to flow naturally with the curves of her body, creating something as unique as she was.

It wasn't his usual sort of work, but it was pretty damn beautiful, if he did say so himself.

Still, he forgot all about her tattoo when he got her panties all the way off.

The softer shades that colored the skin and hair the lingerie had been hiding were even more striking, and it was impossible to look away. She obviously took pains to keep the triangle of dark hair above her pussy neatly groomed. He stroked a thumb over its surface—it was surprisingly soft.

Her skin below was even softer, slick with moisture. He stroked her clit, leaning in to kiss her again at the same time.

As their lips met, she opened her thighs wider, her breath rushing against his face before their mouths were sealed together.

He took advantage of the wider space between her legs, stepping between them. His cock ached, hard beneath his jeans, uncomfortable against the zipper. He'd be in agony for the rest of the day, without a doubt. But it'd be worth it just to hear her moan again, to see her experience pleasure that defied her usual silence and know it was because of him.

That particular wish was fulfilled within seconds. As he touched her clit, establishing a rhythm and teasing the slick skin below with his other hand, a moan rose from her chest, making his lips tingle and his dick harden even more.

He slipped a finger inside her, unable to resist the promise of heat and pressure, the lure of being inside her, even if it was only like this.

Hot and tight, her body welcomed him with a squeeze he felt all the way down in his jeans, even though he was fully clothed and she was gripping the edge of the table with both hands.

He added another finger, delving deeper in search of a certain spot. When she tossed her head back, ending their kiss without catching her breath, it seemed like he'd found it.

He kept doing what he was doing, fingers hot inside her and on her clit, growing slicker by the second.

She squeezed her eyes shut, but he kept his wide open, gaze roving all over her body, taking in everything from the flush that'd spread across her face to the sight of his own fingers disappearing into her pussy, lost in soft flesh.

He was closer to coming than he'd been in too long, his entire body tense with desire that ate at him from the inside out, on a hair-trigger. If she so much as touched him—

The sound of another moan shattered his thoughts, followed by hard breathing. She arched and her body went tight around his fingers, squeezing. He could just imagine that perfect pressure surrounding his cock, that perfect body under and against his...

Her pussy drew even tighter and he breathed hard too, losing all the air in his lungs as the fantasy threatened to strangle what was left of his good sense. In that moment, he'd never regretted anything more than he regretted his lack of contraception.

As her breathing slowed, less irregular but still shaky, reality slammed down on him and he finally pulled his hands from her body.

"Gonna be late," he said, dragging his gaze from Arianna and glancing reluctantly at the clock instead. "I've gotta go."

When he looked back down at her, he saw that she held one hand still in the air, halfway between her body and his. Her fingertips were mere inches from his dick.

He barely suppressed a groan. The thought of reciprocation hadn't been what'd driven him to do what he just had, but now that the idea had taken hold, it was painful in its intensity. He would've given almost anything just to feel her hand wrapped around his shaft for even a second, but if he let her so much as brush her fingertips across his cock, there'd be no way he'd be able to make himself leave.

He had a client waiting, a reputation to uphold. Plus Jed would give him hell if he didn't keep his appointment, and rightfully so. He fought to remind himself why those things were important while his mind swam in a fog of unfulfilled desire.

"Right now?" Arianna asked, still half-naked, her thighs open wide enough to allow him to stand between them.

He forced himself to take a step backward. "Yeah."

As he handed her her jeans and panties, reality came slowly back into focus. He really would be late if he didn't hurry the fuck up, but Emily was still asleep in her swing in the living room. That small miracle tempted him to stay, to lay hands on Arianna again and refuse to let go until he absolutely had to.

"I'll see you tonight," Arianna said.

"Yeah, you will." His dick twitched against his jeans. He couldn't fucking wait.

* * * * *

Arianna sank down into a chair at the kitchen table – the same chair she'd been sitting in when James had kissed her. She'd spent several panty-melting moments there before he'd lifted her onto the table where her elbow rested now, beside a cup of herbal tea.

She was completely hopeless. She couldn't stop thinking about him. What he'd done to her kept playing on a loop inside her head, and she found herself aching and tingling along with the memories, in all the places he'd touched her.

She sipped the tea, which she'd chosen instead of coffee. Caffeine was the last thing she needed right now. She was still wired from her encounter with James. Woven into all the tantalizing thoughts that raced through her mind was the knowledge that he'd be back in just a few hours. Would they pick up where they'd left off?

She glanced toward the swing in the living room, where Emily was napping again. If she happened to be asleep when James arrived, maybe things would start with another kiss and take off from there. Arianna didn't have any condoms, and without a stroller or car seat, she couldn't go out to buy any. Even if James didn't think to pick any up, he'd proven that there were other things they could do. She wouldn't mind getting her hands on him, next time around.

Just the thought was enough to send a shiver down her spine, one that was more hot than cold. He'd surprised her with what he'd done. When he'd told her not to worry about not having protection, she'd frozen, stunned into disappointment so deep it'd hurt. In that moment, she'd felt the familiar shame of having misjudged, of discovering that she meant less to someone than she could've imagined.

But she'd been wrong. When she'd realized what he'd really meant, she'd felt a different sort of shame – shame over having misjudged *him*. And then she'd forgotten about anything remotely like shame as he'd given her pleasure so hot it'd melted away any attempts at second-guessing what they were doing.

The feeling lingered now, hours later, and was intoxicating.

She nearly dropped her teacup when her phone rang. Jasmine-scented water sloshed over the rim, falling to the tabletop in a smattering of hot droplets. She ignored the mess in favor of hurrying to the counter, silencing her phone before the ringtone could wake Emily up.

"Hello?" She didn't even take time to glance at the screen before answering.

"Arianna."

"Selena?" She recognized her older sister's voice, though they hadn't spoken in weeks.

"Yeah, it's me. How are you?"

Arianna's heart raced, each beat a reminder of the secret pleasure that glowed inside her like a small sun. "Good. What about you?"

"I'm fine. Listen, I'm calling because—"

Emily whined, and the sound was quickly followed by a longer wail. The fact that she was in the next room didn't matter much; Selena's words were drowned out by the crying. Apparently, Arianna hadn't answered her phone quickly enough.

"Hold on," she said. "I've got to put my phone down for a minute."

Emily wasn't happy about having been woken up early. Her face was red and her little fists were clenched when Arianna lifted her out of her swing. It took a minute of holding her, rocking lightly, to calm her down.

When Arianna picked her phone back up with one hand, she held Emily against her chest with the other. "I'm back."

"Is that a *baby* in the background?" Selena said it like it was so crazy she almost couldn't believe it.

"Yeah."

For several seconds, Selena didn't say anything.

"I'm babysitting for a friend," Arianna said, begrudging Selena the truth.

"Oh. Well, actually I was calling to see if you'd be willing to babysit for me."

Now it was Arianna's turn not to say anything as she did her best to shift Emily into a more comfortable position, wary of provoking another bout of crying.

"They changed my work schedule around next week – my immediate supervisor is taking some time off to have surgery. They asked me to fill in, and it's going to mean working some extra hours. Mom would've watched Maya, but she and dad are going on vacation next week."

"Right. The Poconos, for their anniversary." Arianna's mother had mentioned something about it to her last time they'd spoken, a few weeks ago.

"Yeah. My shifts next week will overlap with Josh's, so we'll really need a babysitter. So … would you mind, Arianna? I know you don't like babysitting much, but it'd only be a few days, and I can pay you if you want."

Arianna gripped the phone more tightly, feeling like a cat that'd just had its fur rubbed backwards. "I never said I didn't like babysitting."

"You don't have to *say* it, and I don't blame you. Look, I wouldn't ask, but filling in for my supervisor is a huge opportunity for me. I don't want to turn it down, and I know you're always home, so…"

Now Arianna felt like a cat that'd had a bucket of cold water dumped over its head. Why did people assume that just because she worked at home, she was always available to do the things they were too busy to do themselves? Working at home meant *working* at home, not watching TV in her sweats all day, or however Selena thought she spent her time.

Still, Arianna liked her sweet one year old niece and didn't spend much time with her, considering that they lived in the same city. She'd only babysat her a handful of times – already, she'd spent more time caring for Emily than Maya. Her relationships with her sister and parents weren't the best of the best, but there was no reason not to try with her niece.

Well, no reason she couldn't overcome, if she put her mind to it and left the past where it belonged: in the past.

"It'll cut into my workdays, but I'll watch her for you," she said. "What times will you be dropping her off and picking her up? Never mind. I can't write anything down – my hands are full. Just text me."

The conversation ended shortly thereafter – something Arianna was grateful for. Although she didn't want to exclude herself from her niece's life, she couldn't help but wonder if she'd done the smart thing by agreeing to watch her. An uneasy feeling in the pit of her stomach flared up every time she imagined Selena dropping off her daughter.

Why did she feel so much worse about watching Maya than Emily?

A million reasons popped into her head. For one, James didn't act like Arianna had nothing better to do and should babysit for him just because. He actually felt bad about infringing on her workday. That fact alone meant that Arianna didn't mind the extra demand on her time at all.

And then there was the fact that though tiny Emily certainly stirred up some emotions Arianna would rather avoid, feeling like she was helping the baby girl, not to mention James, kept most of the pain at bay. With Maya...

It was different. Maybe it shouldn't have been, but it was. The little girl was sweet as sugar, but Selena could be grating and it'd been ten years since Arianna's relations with her immediate family had been smooth. They rarely talked about the event that'd caused a deep rift years ago, but they'd never been as close since then, either.

Relationships could be scarred, just like people.

Arianna let her free hand drift over the front of her body, her fingertips skimming her belly and resting on her hip. Beneath her clothing was ink James had put in her skin, and beneath that, something much less beautiful. She'd changed over the past decade, but deep down, she was still marked by what she'd endured. Hiding it didn't change anything.

Emily raised her fist to her lips, making a serious effort to fit it inside her mouth.

Arianna turned to the counter, surprised at how natural it felt to cradle a baby against her shoulder while she made a bottle one-handedly. She'd fallen into the routine of caring for a newborn quickly, and recognizing that fact sent her spiraling even deeper into uncertainty.

* * * * *

When the sound of knocking echoed through Arianna's apartment, it was late. Glancing at the clock, she realized just how late, and hurried to the door.

James stood there in all his glory, and the sight of him snapped her out of the melancholy mood she'd been in for the past few hours. Thoughts of Selena and the past flew out the window as James' grey-green eyes locked with hers, pulling her thoroughly into the present. Her entire body heated up as she remembered the feeling of his lips against hers, his hands on her body, inside her…

It seemed like it'd been an eternity since he'd pushed her to climax right on top of her kitchen table early that afternoon. At the same time, it felt like no time had passed at all.

"Hey," he said, stepping inside. "How'd the rest of your day go?"

The rest of your day. Arianna's body temperature seemed to creep a few degrees higher as she turned his words over in her mind, reading between them.

"There's not much to say. It wasn't bad, but it was all downhill after lunchtime."

His lips curled faintly, giving in to a smile that threatened to melt her panties off.

This was the James she'd been so excited to get to know after her last tattoo, during dinner and on their way to his apartment. Over the past week, she'd discovered there was more to him than staggering sex appeal, but she certainly wasn't complaining about the reemergence of his seductive side. Especially not after what'd happened that afternoon.

"It was the same way for me," he said, stepping closer to her, just barely infringing on her personal space. "But I have a feeling things are about to look up."

A thrill rippled through Arianna. Somehow, he always looked hotter in real life than she remembered. Memory was two-dimensional; when he was really in front of her, she couldn't help but stare, mentally cataloging all the sexy details her mind's eye just couldn't do justice. The strong line of his jaw, the rare golden shade of his hair and the even more unusual color of his eyes... Even up close, she couldn't decide whether they were more grey or green.

"Emily's napping," she said, nodding toward the swing, "but I don't know how much longer it'll last. She's been out for about 20 minutes now." She could nap for another hour, or wake up at any moment. Trying to get amorous while a sleeping baby was in the apartment seemed like a game of

Russian roulette – if she woke up too soon, their plans would be shot down.

But it was either take a gamble, or simply forego what might have been. The look in James' eyes said that he found the latter idea just as unbearable as she did.

"Hopefully it'll last long enough," he said, reaching for her.

His hands settled on her hips, and it was like picking up where they'd left off. Beneath the pressure of his, her lips felt faintly bruised from their earlier kiss. It was a good kind of hurt though – the kind that let her know she was alive. This was the sort of thrill it'd been worth coming out of her shell for.

The thought rushed through her, buoying her confidence as James slid his tongue between her lips.

As their kiss deepened, he gripped her hips more tightly.

She reciprocated by placing her hands on his body, first on his chest and then below, letting her palms glide over his stomach. He was smooth and flat there, his body radiating heat that warmed her through the thin fabric of his t-shirt. Then her hands hit his jeans, rough denim already strained over the hard rod of his erection.

Her heart skipped a beat as her fingertips brushed the rounded head of his cock, easily discernible, even with his clothing in the way. It was trapped tight against his body – any higher and it'd be jutting out of his jeans altogether.

The thought made her tingle all over.

When she ran the pad of her thumb down the length of his shaft, he broke their kiss with a hard breath, leaning back. His gaze drifted to the kitchen and the table where they'd last touched, then focused on her.

"I stopped at the store on my way here." He dipped a hand into one of his jeans pockets.

The sight of the square package he held aloft made her breath catch in her lungs. Realizing that they'd finally get what they'd set their hearts on a week ago, she felt almost giddy. If anything, her desire for him had increased since then – tenfold, at least.

"Great," she said, her gaze drawn to the table too.

When she looked back at James, he locked her in eye contact as intense as their last kiss.

"I've got a bed, you know. And I'm not sure that table was made for what we're planning." It'd been a cheap department store purchase, and though it'd supported her well enough earlier that day, James' look of pure lust made her doubt the wisdom of expecting it to hold up to whatever would come next.

He gripped one of her hands, suddenly and fiercely, squeezing her fingers. "I can tell you now that that table was never meant to stand up to what I want to do to you."

Her heart beat so hard she was almost afraid he'd hear it. "Come on."

CHAPTER 7

Leading him by the hand to her bedroom felt daring, and more natural – more right – than she could've imagined. Maybe the promise she'd made herself was already coming true; maybe she was becoming bolder. The idea was satisfying, but for reasons other than those she'd expected. Now that it was actually happening, she knew deep down that she didn't want to simply walk away from this with boosted confidence and a little more experience.

She didn't particularly care if being with James broadened her horizons. She liked *this* situation, as strange as it was, and memories wouldn't be enough to sustain a semblance of happiness. Not when it came to him.

He reinforced what she was already sure of by wrapping his arms around her as soon as they entered her bedroom. She didn't even see the full-sized bed with its purple comforter, or the bookshelf by the window. She could've been anywhere; her eyes were tightly shut, and the feel and taste of him overwhelmed her, wiping awareness of anything else from her mind.

His grip on her hips was firm. He held her to him as he slipped his tongue into her mouth, delving deep.

Her breasts ached as they were compressed against his chest, and she was teased by phantom pressure in her core, a reminder of what he'd done hours ago. He'd already been inside her, had already seen and touched more of her than she'd exposed to anyone in a long time. She, on the other hand, had only fantasized about exploring him like that.

He groaned when she pressed her hand against the front of his jeans, palming his hard-on, eager to feel him skin-to-skin. Time was of the essence, but she doubted she'd have been able to slow down even if that hadn't been the case. She'd already been waiting for more than a week, and it felt like it'd been even longer than that. Now that it was finally happening, she couldn't keep her hands off him.

He seemed to feel the same way about her. His hands roved all over her body, gliding over her belly and breasts, slipping beneath the hem of her t-shirt. In a matter of moments, he'd stripped that over her head and was grasping the clasp of her bra.

When her bra was tossed aside, the feel of his hands on her bare breasts stole her breath away. Freezing with her fingers still touching the hard length of his erection, she took a moment to gather her thoughts before launching into action.

Last time, he'd stripped her down to almost nothing, had explored all the most intimate parts of her while exposing nothing of himself. She didn't begrudge him that – it'd been the most erotic thing she'd experienced in well … ever – but there was no way that was happening again. Gripping the waistband of his jeans in both hands, she let a thumb drift over the cool surface of a brass button.

When she unzipped his pants, he ended their kiss and breathed hard into her hair, still cupping her breasts, squeezing. His dick rose immediately from the confines of his clothing, the shaft standing tall between the parted teeth of the zipper, head straining a last layer of cotton.

She stared at the promising shape, so close she could almost feel the smooth heat of him against her fingertips. Slipping a hand into his boxer-briefs, she freed him.

He was everything she'd expected from the moment her fingertips had first brushed the stiff rod of his cock. Smooth and hot to the touch, so hard that everything inside her drew up tight when she let her hand glide over his shaft. Everything she'd anticipated, except...

Well, there was a little something extra. Apparently, he hadn't been joking about being pierced. Gleaming silver and stark against his skin was a captive bead, the steel loop disappearing into his flesh just over the base of his cock. Above the piercing, hair as blond as that on his head didn't detract from the jewelry.

When she met his eyes, a wicked smile played across his lips. "Told you," he said.

In the heated moments since he'd walked through the door, she'd forgotten all about the mystery of whether he was really pierced or not. Feeling him through his jeans hadn't given any indication, either – whenever she thought of guys being pierced down there, she imagined jewelry inserted through the head of their cock, maybe even the shaft. This was different...

"I've never seen a piercing like that before." And she'd certainly never seen a piercing of any sort on a guy this up-close and personal.

"It's less about how it looks and more about how it feels."

Heat blazed a trail across her cheekbones. "I like how it looks."

She did. The sight of hard steel against tender flesh created an erotic paradox, one she could feel working its way through her veins in the form of white-hot lust.

"I'm glad." His grin widened, and he gave her breasts another squeeze, supporting them from below as he teased her nipples with his fingertips.

Her breath got caught somewhere between her lungs and her lips, rendering her mute. The way he was touching her felt almost as good as the tabletop treatment he'd given her – beneath his fingertips, her skin was so sensitive she could hardly stand it.

"Did it hurt?" The words tumbled out as her thoughts bled into a haze, becoming less and less coherent.

"The piercing?"

She nodded, and the top of her head brushed his jaw. Even that felt sexy.

"Wasn't that bad," he said. "Even if it had been, it'd be worth it, because it's not going to hurt you – just the opposite."

A frisson zipped down her spine. "What do you mean?"

"Let me show you."

Before she even realized what he was doing, he pulled the condom out of his pocket and tore the foil.

"Wait," she said, her heart in her throat.

His raised his gaze to meet hers. "What?"

"Your clothes… Take them off. I want to see you, this time." Her pulse rocketed as she raked her gaze over his body, imagining what lay beneath. "What's the point of all those tattoos if you're not going to show them off?"

He returned her smile, but there was a hard look of lust in his eyes that didn't soften.

To her relief, he complied, tearing away his shirt before she could so much as draw another breath.

When she laid eyes on what his clothing had been hiding, she remained breathless for several more moments.

His torso was inked, which came as no surprise considering the fact that even his hands were tattooed. She let her gaze drift over the designs, focusing on the twin swallows below his collarbones. When he stripped off his jeans, she was half-surprised to discover that the lower half of his body wasn't tattooed.

No matter how decorated his body was, no amount of ink or steel could distract the eye from how badly he obviously wanted her. More rigid than ever, his cock drew her gaze and her hand.

She gripped his shaft, thumbing the blunt curve of the head before sliding down, letting her fist drift all the way to the root of his dick, where the captive bead kissed the edge of her palm.

He exhaled hard, breath smelling like coffee and mint. The combination was sweet and bold, a temptation. Arianna leaned into him, tilting her head back so that her lips brushed his.

He crushed his mouth to hers and slid his hands from her breasts, wrapping his arms around her instead. Her head spun, and for a second she thought it was a side-effect of the kiss. Then she realized she was halfway airborne, still in James' arms, but with her feet no longer touching the floor.

Before she knew it, she was sinking into the mattress, the soft comforter against her back. Even better, James was on top of her. Her hand had slipped from around his thick shaft, and now that same hardness pressed against her belly. Somehow, he'd ended up between her thighs.

A shiver of delight raced down her spine – if only she hadn't been wearing her jeans.

Something scratched her side where he was touching her, a sharp contrast to the feel of his skin against hers.

Glancing down, she saw it was the condom package – he was still holding it.

Rising to his knees, he looked like he was about to finish what he'd started to do while they'd still been standing. Instead, he dropped the package, laying his hands on her hips instead.

He had her jeans unbuttoned and unzipped in the blink of an eye. Several breathless seconds later, they were off altogether. Her panties were next to go, whisked off her hips and over her ankles as he swore softly under his breath, eyes shining with a look that had to be mirrored on her own face.

Bare beneath him, with her thighs spread and his body between them, she couldn't remember ever wanting anything so badly. He was so hard, and as he rolled the condom on, fingers sliding down the sides of his shaft and coming to a halt by the jewelry above, her heart skipped a beat.

She'd fantasized so many times about this, about being with him. At Hot Ink, while he'd been tattooing her, and at home, when she'd been unable to shake the desire that he'd left her with, seemingly just as permanent as the ink in her skin. But her mind hadn't been able to fabricate this degree of desire, or the way a never-ending shiver seemed to zip up and down her spine, causing her body to tingle all over, rendering her skin hyper-sensitive as her nerve endings sizzled beneath the surface.

The memory of his touch left her feeling drugged, and the anticipation of feeling it again leant a sharper edge to the sensation.

When he really did touch her, it was with the head of his dick. Lowering himself over her, he guided it with one hand, pressing hot, hard flesh against her clit.

The moment of contact stole her breath away. The condom was only a thin layer, and she could feel his heat and hardness through it. When he rubbed himself against her that way, it felt even better than the way he'd touched her in the kitchen.

Still, she ached to have him inside her. He was so close; each second that ticked by without him pressing inside her was torture. Sweet torture that was just as good as it was agonizing, but still – she was glad when he finally slid a little lower, teasing the lips of her pussy.

Her skin was slick and he slid inside easily, stretching her inch by inch. It had been a while since she'd been with anybody, and as he filled her, she could hardly remember the last time, or any other time, really – a fact she appreciated. He felt better inside her than anyone else ever had, especially when he was buried to the root and the piece of jewelry there pressed against her clit.

It's less about how it looks and more about how it feels. What he'd said made sense now. Hard against her sensitive bud, the captive bead made it feel like he was still touching her externally, adding an extra thrill to the sheer bliss of penetration.

It was almost too much to process all at once. Almost. Her inner muscles drew up tight, embracing his shaft.

He sighed, breath hot against her cheek. "Been thinking about this all day."

She sighed too and when he rocked his hips, her sigh bled into a moan. Each thrust provided a dual burst of pleasure, the back-to-back sensations of internal and external friction. And on top of that – on top of her – there was the view: James' body, a temple of defined muscle decorated with ink that set it all off. Looking up at him was definitely the hottest thing she'd ever seen.

He looked back down at her like he couldn't look away either, and the thought cut through Arianna like a hot knife through butter, melting her from the inside out. In that moment, it seemed ludicrous that she'd ever doubted this would happen. How had they waited so long, and how would they keep their hands off each other after this?

He rocked her, supporting himself against the mattress on his elbows, biceps bulging faintly beneath dark ink. She saw stars – literally; they trailed down one arm, inked there permanently – and then it became difficult to focus on anything as he thrust harder. When he said her name, the sound of his voice broke her concentration completely.

She met his eyes for half a moment before shutting them, tilting her head back against the pillow and focusing on the tension mounting in her core. Every time the head of his cock delved deep, forcing her softer flesh to yield to his, she was thrust one step closer to the edge. The pressure of the bead rocking against her clit nearly pushed her to climax every time. A little more, and she'd be there.

She wrapped her arms around his neck, unable to resist pulling him a little closer. He kissed her, still tasting like coffee and mint.

Her climax crashed down on her as her tongue twined with his. Shrinking, her pussy drew tight as contractions swept through her core, leaving her even more breathless than the pressure of his mouth against hers had.

He kissed her harder, fucked her harder.

Her moan got lost somewhere between her lips and his.

Whenever she began to come down from the peak he'd pushed her to, she realized she'd gone from embracing him to clinging to him, her nails anchored in his shoulders. Before she had a chance to let go, he gathered her up in his arms, muscles shifting beneath their cover of ink as he held her close.

When his lips cracked, it seemed like he might kiss her again. Instead, he sighed, breath escaping along with a ragged sound that sparked fresh lust inside her. They were so close she could feel his heart beating, and when he came, she felt that too.

Every muscle in his body grew a little more tense, and his grey-green irises disappeared beneath the sweep of blond lashes. Inside her, he was harder than ever, thrusting with enough force to make the bed shake beneath them.

Or maybe she was trembling. It was hard to tell, he was holding her so tightly. Him coming inside her felt so good she might've shattered into a million little pieces if he hadn't been cradling her like that.

He didn't pull out right away. For a few moments, he stayed hard, stayed inside her. "So good," he said when he finally eased out of her, sitting up on the bed beside her, his hip touching hers. "Do you think…"

Several silent seconds ticked by, and she used them to find her voice. "What?"

He met her eyes, locking her in eye contact that nearly stopped her heart. His gaze was intense, and his lips were swollen from being pressed so long and hard against hers. "Do you think we have time to do it again?"

His words went straight through her as she turned onto her side and pushed herself up into a sitting position. "Right now?" The idea was electrifying, though they'd already been lucky in that Emily hadn't woken from her nap yet.

"Yeah. Unless you don't want to. I know that could've lasted longer, but I didn't know how long we had and I couldn't stand the thought of having to stop. You were too perfect, and it felt too good. I think it might've killed me to have to leave here without finishing."

Heat swept over her from head to toe, and she could only hope he wouldn't notice the blush. Her skin wasn't as fair as his – unmissable patches of color had spread across his face, highlighting his sculpted cheekbones.

"It was perfect the way it was," she said, biting the tip of her tongue. She'd had an orgasm – an amazing one – and it was her second of the day. Sadly, that was more than she could credit to any other guy she'd been with in the past – with anyone else, she would've counted herself lucky to have just one. What would James think if he knew that?

Wondering embarrassed her. A decade ago, Cody had more or less crippled her ability to trust a sexual partner, which had stunted her experience right out of the starting gate. Afterward, it'd taken her years to get to the point where she was comfortable enough to even be capable of having an orgasm during sex.

James, on the other hand, had apparently had his genitals pierced for the sole purpose of clitoral stimulation. No doubt her past sex life was lame compared to his.

"Yeah?" His lips quirked in a half-smile. "So does that mean you wouldn't be averse to giving it another try?" He ran a hand up her leg, his fingertips brushing her inner thigh.

Her nipples hardened in instant response.

He must've noticed. Cupping one of her breasts, he stroked the stiff peak with his thumb.

"Not averse, no. But we might get interrupted." Would trying for a second round of incredible sex be pushing their luck? Maybe, but the lure of doing just that was undeniably tempting.

"We might." He leaned in, brushing his lips across the arch of her neck. "But right now we've got time on our hands, and when that's the case, I don't think I can keep my hands off you."

Her gaze drifted south, to his groin. Amazingly, he was still erect. The sight of him so ready for more after what they'd just done was irresistible, and she couldn't help but notice that the jewelry above the base of his dick shone more brightly than before – it was wet.

So was she, even after the best sex of her life.

"I've got another condom," he breathed. "I'll switch out."

Her core clenched as longing gripped her. "Okay. And if we have to stop… Maybe you could stay here tonight. You and Emily. I'm sure you and I would have a chance to pick up where we left off eventually if you stuck around."

He raised his head, meeting her eyes. "You mean that – you really want me to stay overnight?"

"Yes." Just the thought filled her with anticipation and a sense of deep satisfaction that was somehow separate from the physical gratification her climax had left her with.

The bed shifted beneath them as he leaned even closer, lowering his face to her breast and capturing her nipple between his lips.

She shut her eyes, reveling in the knowledge that he'd be staying. He'd be hers for the entire night – reality was turning out even better than she'd dared to fantasize.

* * * * *

Waking up was like being dragged to the surface of deep water after a long submersion. James drew a deep breath, stretching limbs that ached, too weighed down with sleep to move efficiently. And then he realized that the deep breath he'd taken had filled his lungs with the scent of lavender.

Lavender? He turned his head, cheek sliding against the pillowcase, and the aroma intensified, released from the fabric.

He'd never done anything to make his pillows smell like lavender. Hell, he was lucky if he remembered to wash the cases every week. Or two.

A distant squawk snapped him into full consciousness, tripping an internal alarm that sent something like fear slipping into his system. Why had the cry come from so far away? He extended an arm, reaching for Emily's bassinette.

It wasn't beside his bed.

Or maybe it was, but he wasn't in *his* bed.

"Fuck," he muttered, swinging his legs over the side of the mattress, limbs flailing.

His attempt at a quick escape took a turn for disaster as the sheet tangled around his ankle, drawing tight. He slipped over the side of the bed and hit the carpet with a *thud*.

"James?" A female voice called from somewhere he couldn't see – a familiar voice.

"Yeah," he called back, his own voice rasping through his dry mouth as he struggled to free himself from the twisted bedclothes.

Arianna appeared in the bedroom doorway just in time to see him flailing his way free of her sheets. She held Emily cradled in one arm and a half-empty bottle in the other.

"Don't let her see me like this," he said, uncomfortably aware that the only thing he was wearing was the steel ring above his dick. "It's – it's creepy as hell." He grabbed a fistful of sheet and held it balled in front of his groin as he stood.

Arianna laughed. "She just finished eating – she's half asleep now. Her eyes aren't even open."

Arianna's eyes were sure as hell open. She stood staring, her gaze lingering … everywhere.

He shot a similar look back at her just because he could. She wasn't naked, but he could see her nipples beneath the thin blue cami she'd worn to bed, and her cotton shorts showed a lot of leg. A little bit of her ass cheeks, too, when she turned around.

His cock stirred beneath the wadded-up sheets.

"I've gotta stick the rest of this in the fridge," Arianna said, raising the bottle as she retreated to the kitchen. "I have a feeling she'll want to finish it soon. Breakfast is on the table, by the way."

There was a clock on top of Arianna's dresser – the sight of it almost stopped James' heart. Eleven o'clock? He couldn't remember the last time he'd slept in so late. He had to be at work in an hour, and being late wasn't an option – his first appointment was booked for noon.

He pulled on his underwear and jeans in a hurry, then rushed out into the kitchen.

"Fuck, I'm sorry, Arianna. You should've just kicked my ass out of bed. How long have you been up with her?"

Arianna shook her head as she put Emily down in her swing. "It doesn't matter. This is the first time you've had a chance to sleep in for nearly two weeks."

"That shouldn't be your problem." There were two places set at the table. He didn't have time for breakfast, but the sight of a full cup of coffee was irresistible. He gripped the mug and raised it to his mouth.

The coffee lapped against his lips, so cold it might as well have been tap water. He barely resisted the urge to spit out the sip he'd taken.

"Oh God," Arianna laughed. "Let me heat that up for you. And your food... By the way, 'breakfast' might've been an exaggeration. I started out wanting to cook something, but somehow that turned into making instant oatmeal in the microwave. I hope you like strawberries and cream."

He set down the cold coffee. "I appreciate it, but I've really gotta go. My first appointment is in an hour." His gut twisted with guilt. First he'd kept her up for the better part of the night, then he'd slept half the day, leaving her to take care of Emily. Now he was about to leave her alone with her for the rest of the day.

Arianna turned, directing her gaze at the clock above the kitchen stove. "Eleven already?" She frowned. "Time goes by fast when you're getting spit up on."

James winced. "Sorry about that. I feel like shit for running out on you like this." Especially after what they'd done. Even now, a part of him – a semi-erect part of him, thanks to her skimpy pajamas – ached to stay with her. His sexual appetite didn't seem to know any end with her.

Still, even just holding her would've been nice.

It'd been a hell of a long time since he'd woken up in someone else's apartment and had that thought. "Listen, Arianna—"

"Don't worry about it," she said. "I'll see you tonight. And feel free to take a rain check on the cold coffee and store brand oatmeal."

He got ready for work, pulling on his shirt, shoes and jacket before grabbing his keys from the kitchen counter. He didn't have much of a choice, though that fact didn't do much to make it feel any less wrong. Especially since as he walked out the door, he thought he heard Arianna sigh – an unhappy sound so different from the noises she'd been making all night that he wondered whether she'd be glad to see him when he returned after the end of his work day.

The thought that she might not be left him feeling just as cold as the coffee he'd turned down.

* * * * *

9 Years Ago

It was cold. Freezing, actually, but James didn't dare turn on the car to run the heat. He only had a quarter of a tank of gas left, and it'd be two more weeks before he got his first paycheck from his new job. Until then, he had exactly fifty-two dollars and six cents to make it on. He shoved his hands deeper into his hoodie's front pocket, rubbing the bills and coins between his fingers, clenching them in his fist. Touching the money was a small comfort and a huge temptation. He could buy more gas, or food…

He did neither. Instead, he reclined the driver's seat all the way and closed his eyes, shutting out the glare of streetlight.

Sleep didn't come easily. In fact, it didn't come at all. His muscles ached from construction work and his stomach felt pinched from hunger. It was hard to imagine making it through two weeks of living in his car during a Pittsburgh November, but he didn't have much of a choice. It'd be at least that long before he'd have the money to put down a deposit on an apartment, and he didn't have enough to stay at a motel meanwhile.

If only things had lasted longer with Chelsea. He'd met her a couple months ago at a party. At first, she'd liked him enough to let him stay with her at her apartment. Still, she'd kicked him out quick the day before when her old boyfriend had come back around.

James had barely had time to gather up his few belongings. She hadn't cared that he started a new job the next day, that it paid a little higher than his last gig. He'd offered to give her all the extra pay to put toward household expenses, but she hadn't cared about that, either.

"It's been fun," she'd said to him, "but I need you to get out before Sean gets here. No offense."

He couldn't say he missed her, but he sure as hell missed her cramped studio apartment, even if the roof had leaked when it rained.

After an hour of lying still inside his piece of shit car, James' will snapped. He turned the key in the ignition and flipped the heat on. Just for a minute or two, until he was warm enough to sleep…

He held his hands up in front of the heating vents, but only cold air came out. He let the vehicle run longer, but the air never warmed up.

"Fuck," he said, striking the dash with one fist. "Fuck it." He climbed out of the car and slammed the door shut before turning on his heel and striding down the sidewalk.

He stopped when he reached a particular hole in the wall, a place where he knew no one would bother to check his ID and see that he wasn't quite 21. The heavy stubble on his jaw and shadows under his eyes made him look older than he really was — not that anyone here would give a shit if they knew his real age, anyway.

He shoved the money he'd been clutching in his fist deep into a jeans pocket, resigned to spending it. Maybe only some of it, if he found the right woman and laid it on thick enough to leave the bar within the next hour. Inside, he knew he'd be able to find someone — some place — to stay with, even if it was just for the night. A stranger's bed would offer cold comfort that'd be better than freezing his ass off in his car. He might even get a little sleep.

CHAPTER 8

Arianna's heart leapt when someone knocked on the door. It had a way of doing that lately, even though as she glanced at the clock, she realized it was way too early for it to be James. It was eight thirty in the morning; she'd only been up for about fifteen minutes. Hot Ink wasn't even open this early.

"Coming," she called, abandoning her half-finished coffee. No, it wouldn't be him at the door, but she did know who was knocking. And she couldn't help but be disappointed.

She hadn't stopped thinking about James since the day before – not for a single moment. Their night together had been burnt into the pleasure-receiving center of her brain; spending the previous night alone had seemed incredibly lame, in comparison. She'd almost asked him to stay again, but it'd been early evening when he'd come to pick up Emily after work, and the supplies of diapers and formula in his bag had nearly been depleted anyway.

Arianna opened the door, nodding to her sister. "Hey, Selena."

Selena wore her brunette hair in a high knot and stood with a toddler balanced on one hip and a diaper bag slung over her shoulder.

"Hey." She stepped inside without hesitating. "Thanks for agreeing to watch Maya an extra day for me. Upper management asked my immediate supervisor to come in today and give me a mini training session on how to handle her job while she's gone. I'm kind of excited – I mean, you never know, it could eventually turn into something permanent."

"You're welcome." Selena's excitement didn't lift Arianna's restless mood.

Maya's big brown eyes did, though. She blinked at Arianna, even cuter than the last time she'd seen her.

"Hey, Maya." She flashed the toddler a smile – hopefully Maya remembered her. "Selena, do you want a cup of coffee or something before you head to work?"

Selena shook her head and pressed Maya into Arianna's arms. "No thanks, I've really gotta go. I'll barely make it there on time as is. Everything you need should be in this bag."

Selena left the diaper bag by the door and was gone seconds later.

"Guess it's just you and me for now, Maya." Arianna locked the door behind Selena. "You'll have a little playmate here in a couple hours, though."

As it turned out, Arianna heard from James before eleven thirty, when he usually dropped off Emily. He called her around ten.

The sight of his name on the screen filled her with instant heat. Her fingertip tingled as she swiped it across the screen, answering his call.

"Hey, I just wanted to let you know that I got Emily set up with a day care center," he said.

"Day care?" The warm feeling began to fade right away.

"Yeah. I know it wasn't fair of me to keep sticking her with you. I appreciate you putting up with me, but I couldn't keep asking you to do that. She's starting at the day care place today."

"I really didn't mind watching her."

"It's only right," he said. "It was tough to find a place that didn't have a waiting list, but it's for the best."

The best? James honestly thought that dropping a month-old baby off at a facility where she'd be one of dozens of kids assigned to a handful of caretakers was better than leaving Emily with her? The thought had her biting her lip, resisting the urge to tell him otherwise.

"So I shouldn't expect to see you at eleven thirty, then?"

"I've gotta drop her off at the day care place instead before I head in to work."

"Right." She couldn't work up the courage to ask him when she could expect to see him next, then. The confidence their time together had instilled in her was too fresh to stand up to this, to old doubts that were much more deeply ingrained.

"Thanks again for helping me out," he said. "I owe you."

The familiar noise of Emily crying sounded in the background.

"Sounds like you've got your hands full," she said. "I hope everything works out okay with the day care." If that was really where he wanted his niece to spend her time while he was at work, it was none of her business. Even if she didn't like it.

Moments later, they said goodbye and Arianna laid her phone back down on the counter. He hadn't mentioned their last time together, or their next. She wasn't sure which stung more: that fact, or that he'd rather leave Emily with strangers than with her.

* * * * *

James steeled himself as he stepped into Jed's office / storage space in the back of Hot Ink. "Look, if this is about me being late today, I know that was lame." He'd walked through the door a half hour late that afternoon and had found his client already waiting on the couch in the reception area. "I'm taking care of my niece and I dropped her off at day care for the first time this morning. When I got there they took me on this long-ass tour and made me fill out paperwork."

Jed shook his head. "Today was the first time you've ever been late. I didn't bring you back here to tear you a new one."

"Then what did you want to talk about?"

Before Jed could reply, the door swung inward, and Karen stepped inside.

"James," she said, beaming, "you're here. Good."

"It's not easy to plan a wedding in just a few weeks," Jed said. "Karen's got to place the final order for tux rentals today. She needs your measurements."

"So you need me to go to the rental place or something?" He buried a tooth in his inner lip. How the hell was he supposed to fit that into his schedule when he had to pick up Emily immediately after work? He'd be arriving close to the day care facility's closing time as it was.

"Actually, I need your measurements right now," Karen said, pulling something out of her pocket. "Don't worry – I looked up how to do this on the internet. I'll just call the rental place here in a minute and give them the numbers."

James stood still in the center of the room as Karen circled him with a measuring tape. He lifted his arms when she asked and didn't mind her running the tape around his chest and up and down his arms to measure for the jacket, pausing periodically to jot down numbers. It was kind of hard to look Jed in the eye though when she bent at the waist to measure him from crotch to heel for the pants.

Likewise when she practically lassoed his ass with the measuring tape, explaining that it was for the "seat" measurement.

"To ensure a proper fit," she said, casting a gaze over her shoulder at her fiancé, "you should be able to fit two fingers between the tape and, uh, James. Could you give me a hand?"

James silently thanked God that Karen hadn't decided to do the test herself. Jed wasn't exactly an overly-emotional guy, but James was pretty sure he wouldn't be enthralled with his fiancée feeling up James' ass in the name of ensuring a perfect fit for his tux.

On the other hand, he also looked reluctant to do it himself. James had seen Jed tattoo people anywhere and everywhere imaginable, but apparently things were different when there was no ink involved. Which made perfect fucking sense. Did Karen really need an ass measurement?

"I've got fingers of my own," James said, shoving two of them between the tape and his hip.

"Perfect," Karen said, and finally released him.

Jed shot James a grateful look.

"Sometimes I ask myself whether there's some way I could limit her internet access," Jed said after Karen strode out of the office, taking her measurements with her. "If I shut off service at the house though, she'd just go to her studio and get online there."

No sooner had the words left his mouth than Karen burst back in, this time carrying a deep purple dress and a small bouquet of roses. "For the bridesmaids," she said, waving the dress. "This one's Mina's. What do you two think of these colors?"

She dissected the bouquet, pulling out flowers one by one and holding them against the dress. There were three altogether, each a different color – white, peach and pink. "I picked up these sample flowers from the florist. Which color compliments the purple best?"

"They all look great to me," Jed said.

James echoed his sentiment.

Karen's eyebrows plunged into a deep V as she narrowed her eyes. "Come on, you guys are artists – I'm counting on your opinions on this."

Several silent moments passed by.

"The peach looks nice," James eventually said.

"Yeah," Jed agreed. "I'd go with either that or the white. But choose whichever you want – I want you to be happy."

"Okay. Peach it is then." She draped the dress over her arm. "Thanks, guys."

She started to leave, then turned. "Here, James, since you spoke up first – enjoy." She thrust the roses at him. "I don't need them anymore."

"Thanks," he said, taking the flowers. "I'll, uh, use them to decorate my booth or something." He could sit them on top of the half wall in a vase.

Only, he didn't have a vase. So when he left Jed's office, he put them in water inside an empty coffee cup instead. The recycled cardboard wasn't exactly the most elegant container, but it worked.

"Hey, James." Jed's voice came from nearby.

James turned to find him standing on the other side of his booth's wall. "Yeah?"

"What with my fiancée measuring your ass, I almost forgot to ask – what was that you were saying about taking care of your niece?"

"My sister dropped her kid off at my apartment," James said, turning his gaze to some hand-drawn art – his work –

hanging on the wall. "And by dropped off, I mean abandoned. Right on my doorstep, just like in a movie."

Jed crossed his arms, frowning. "When did this happen?"

"About a week and a half ago."

"You've been taking care of her this whole time – how old is she?"

"A month old. And yeah. I had some help." He swallowed a knot of guilt that had slipped into his throat, forcing out a half truth. "From a friend. She watched my niece for me while I was at work. I got her set up with a day care center today, though."

Jed swore, a crude phrase that echoed above the sounds of music and the humming noise coming from Tyler's booth as he worked on a client. "Is your sister coming back for her kid?"

"I don't know." James had asked himself that a million times. "I don't have any way of getting in touch with her. She could be on the other side of the world for all I know." It wasn't likely, but he'd considered about a million possible explanations for what Crystal had done.

None of them justified her actions.

"Shit." Jed stood there, glowering.

James nodded. "Yeah. Shit."

"Guess that's why you look like you've been punched in the face, twice," Jed added.

James looked in the mirror that took up most of one wall. Were the dark circles under his eyes really that bad?

"You need some help watching your niece?"

"I've got the day care now," he said, "for while I'm at work." How he'd afford it long-term, he didn't have a fucking clue. He couldn't afford to think long-term, though – it'd be enough to drive him crazy. He just had to make it work, one day at a time. Emily deserved that, at least.

"Yeah, but what about when you're not? If you need a break, Karen and I could help you out – take her for an evening or something."

"You sure about that?" James had known Jed for a long time, and it was hard to picture the guy with baby vomit splattered down the front of his black t-shirt.

"It wouldn't be a big deal. Karen and I have watched Abby's twins quite a few times. Karen likes to photograph them for some project of hers, and to thank Abby for letting her take the pictures, we do some babysitting. Karen thinks it's fun. She'd probably love being around a newborn, especially if you let her photograph the kid."

"If you really mean that, I'd appreciate the hell out of it." Taking care of Emily 24/7 was hard, no doubt about it, but what really motivated him to accept Jed's offer was the thought of Arianna. He'd do just about anything to get some time alone with her.

* * * * *

7 Years Ago

It was a shitty, rainy day. No surprise, since the entire week had been shitty and rainy so far. The springtime thunder storms were so bad that James' construction job had been called off for days, now. Not having any work for a week had churned up a familiar sense of desperation, and it was that god-awful feeling that propelled him through the doors of a place called Hot Ink, even though common sense told him they wouldn't want him.

He'd seen the 'artist wanted' sign in their window the week before, when he'd been walking by on his way to a construction site. He'd immediately thought of his sketchbook full of art – if he could even call it that – and an idea had taken root in his mind. A week of doubting himself hadn't been enough to eradicate it completely.

It felt good to get inside, out of the rain, even if he did feel like a dumbass standing there, dripping on the linoleum.

"Welcome to Hot Ink. Do you have an appointment?" A woman behind a counter bearing a cash register greeted him. She was pretty, with a slight figure and brown hair trimmed in one of those pixie haircuts. Tattoos scrolled up and down her forearms.

"Uh, no." James shook his head, casting a guilty look down at the puddle forming at his feet. "I saw your sign." He tipped his head toward the window. "Are you still looking for someone?"

He braced himself for her rejection. She could probably tell just from looking at him that he didn't know shit about tattooing. Why had he even thought that they might teach him, that being able to draw would mean anything?

She smiled at him. "You should talk to Jed." She turned and peered down the aisle that bisected most of the shop, lined with booths on both sides. "Hey, Jed?"

"Yeah, Alice?" a deep voice called back to her.

"There's an artist here to see you."

He almost said something, almost admitted that he wasn't an artist and didn't have any business being there. Something held him in place though, gluing his feet to the floor as a huge guy covered in tattoos emerged from one of the booths.

The guy shook his hand. "I'm Jed."

"James."

Jed invited him to sit down on a leather couch in what looked like a waiting area. When they were both seated, he asked James about his experience.

James' tongue felt like it was made of cement. What was he supposed to say – that he'd always been good at drawing, that he excelled at delighting his one-night stands by sketching their portraits and leaving the drawings on their nightstands when he left? That art had never really been much more than a hobby and a method of flirtation, an outlet and a party trick that earned him cheap praise… Something to leave behind, something that meant he just might be remembered.

110

He managed to get some bullshit about drawing out, about being interested in tattooing, wanting to learn.

Jed didn't seem impressed. Then again, he didn't kick James out of the shop either, and that was something.

"What do you do for a living?" Jed asked.

James glanced down at his hands – raw knuckles and calloused palms. "Construction."

"You like it?"

"No, but it keeps a roof over my head." Since turning eighteen three years ago, he'd spent enough nights without one of those to appreciate having shelter, having work of any sort.

"I'll be honest with you," Jed said. "I'm looking for an established artist who can help meet the growing demand Hot Ink has seen over the past few months, not someone to teach. And even if I taught you, an apprenticeship takes a long time. How long would depend on how hard you applied yourself, but you could expect it to take at least a year before you'd be ready to actually tattoo anyone."

James didn't know what to say to that. A year didn't seem like that long, when it came to learning how to apply something permanent to somebody's body.

"You'd be expected to stick around here for a while after that, of course," Jed said. "Were you thinking of putting down roots like that when you walked in here?"

Putting down roots. Jed's words cut straight through James, putting down roots of their own somewhere deep in his consciousness. He looked around the tattoo shop and tried to imagine what it would be like to have a place to return to day after day – a place where he belonged. People who knew him, who counted on him being there. Who'd give enough of a damn to get pissed at him if he wasn't.

He glanced at the woman behind the counter, and she smiled at him again. Jed, on the other hand, wore his serious expression like a mask, but he seemed like an all right guy. He was treating James like he deserved to be taken seriously, anyway, when in reality he probably *didn't. "I was hoping for a place to put down roots when I walked in here," James said.*

Now that he thought about it, he realized that was true. If Jed would teach him to tattoo, he'd have work that mattered – something he could take pride in – as well as a place to anchor him in the world. The thought was strangely appealing – almost intoxicating. "If you took me on, I think you'd have a hell of a hard time getting rid of me."

Jed stood up and walked away.

James sat frozen on the couch. Had he said something wrong? He played the conversation over in his head and realized that Jed probably wanted to get rid of him already. James glanced toward the door, at the deluge pouring down outside, slickening the sidewalks and soaking those who dared to brave the streets without an umbrella. A part of him wanted to run, not walk, out the door. Another part of him didn't want to leave at all, didn't want to give up the fantasy of a life with meaning.

Jed was leaning on the counter, talking to the woman behind it. She nodded, said something James couldn't hear and leaned forward, rocking up onto the tips of her toes to press a kiss against Jed's jaw.

Jed returned to the couch. "It takes a lot more work than just tattooing to run a place like this," he said, "and my wife has really had her hands full with it lately. If you want, I'll take you on part-time to help her with administrative work, cleaning and errands – stuff like that. We can work around your construction job schedule, and you can put together a portfolio of your artwork for me. If I think you have enough potential, I'll take you on as an apprentice."

All the doubts tumbling through James' mind stopped, evaporating and leaving him feeling strangely hopeful. "Yeah?"

"I'm not making any promises," Jed said. "For all I know, you can't even draw a stick figure."

"When can I start?"

"You have anywhere else you need to be today?"

"No."

"Then stay. Alice has a whole list of things that need to be done. We won't be closing up shop 'till around midnight tonight, and you can

work until then. Whether or not you come back tomorrow – well, that's up to you."

"I will." He would. Already, he knew in his bones that whatever had possessed Jed to give him a chance was the start of something good – something he'd never had before, and wouldn't want to give up.

* * * * *

"Coming," Arianna called, striding across the living room and to the front door. The short trip had her breathing a little harder than usual – she blamed that on the fact that she'd just spent the past five minutes chasing Maya around the apartment.

The kid could really move. Babysitting a one year old was exhausting, especially compared to watching a newborn. Maya was into anything and everything, running and climbing on deceptively short and chubby little legs. Less than five minutes after her arrival, Arianna had had to give her apartment an emergency childproofing treatment.

That had mostly involved fastening her cabinet doors shut with hair elastics and unplugging her small appliances so that Maya couldn't pull them down by their cords. At some point before Maya came over again, she'd have to buy some plastic plugs for the wall outlets.

"Hey Selena," Arianna said as she pulled open the door, automatically sticking one leg out at an awkward angle so that Maya couldn't rush through the gap and out into the hall.

Maya wrapped herself around Arianna's leg, hugging her kneecap and giggling.

Arianna, on the other hand, was shocked into silence. It wasn't Selena at the door – it was James. He held a small bunch of roses, and other than that, his hands were empty. No diaper bag, no Emily.

"What are you doing here?" she asked as her heart picked up pace.

"I'm here to take you out," he said. "To thank you for everything you've done to help me and Emily out." He pressed the flowers into her hand.

Arianna accepted them, torn between wild happiness and a creeping sense of disappointment. Did he just want to thank her for her help, or was this another date?

"They're gorgeous," she said, stroking the silky petal of a peach-colored rose. "Thanks. I'll put them in the vase with the others – they haven't wilted yet."

James shrugged. "Got them from work and thought of you."

She melted a little inside, despite her doubt. "Where's Emily?"

"Jed and his fiancée Karen are babysitting her for me this evening. Karen's a photographer – loves to take pictures of babies, apparently."

"You finally got an evening all to yourself and you chose to come here?" She melted a little more.

"What the hell would I want with an evening to myself? The first thing I thought of when Jed said they'd watch Emily was that I could finally get some time alone with you." He glanced down at Maya. "If you're not busy."

Arianna felt like skipping. Unfortunately, Maya weighed down her leg like a cement block. "This is my niece, Maya. I'm babysitting her for my sister, but she should be here to pick her up in a few minutes. I'd love to go out with you." She wouldn't have minded staying in with him, either, but hopefully that went without saying.

"It's a date, then."

She raised a brow, her pulse speeding as he met her eyes. "Is it?" She needed to know – needed to make sure. Because if their evening together wasn't going to end in bed –

or on the kitchen table; she wasn't picky – she needed to start steeling herself now for what could otherwise prove to be an unbearable dose of disappointment.

"Flowers. A dinner invitation…" James shook his head. "I thought I was doing everything right now, even if we did start out backwards."

"What do you mean 'everything right'?" Everything they'd done so far had sure as hell *felt* right.

"I mean a guy gives a woman he likes flowers and takes her out to dinner… That's Dating 101, right?"

"You said you were taking me out to show your appreciation. I was just making sure that that wasn't the only reason we're going out." A little pang of guilt sailed through her as she spoke. Obviously, it was a date. The realization buoyed her now, making it impossible not to smile. She'd doubted only moments ago though, her confidence dampened by the fact that James had chosen to entrust Emily to a day care instead of to her.

If only she could press some kind of button to dial back her insecurity. Coming out of her shell was tough – sometimes the temptation to slink back inside was strong, a self-protective instinct. How could she bravely face the possibility of being rejected by James after what they'd done? He'd given her a taste of the sort of sex she'd only heard or read about before – the best of her life. She couldn't lose that so soon.

More importantly, she couldn't lose him.

CHAPTER 9

"I definitely have ulterior motives," he said, "but you deserve a night out, especially after all the hours you've spent shut up in here with my niece."

She bit her tongue before she could blurt out that she normally spent her days shut up inside anyway – it was her job, after all – and that caring for Emily had been a nice change from the norm, especially since it had meant looking forward to seeing him every day.

"How was Emily's first time at day care?" she asked as James stepped inside, closing the door behind himself.

James' expression hardened a little, and he shrugged. "One of the caretakers said she was 'fussy'. I think that means she cried a lot. They said that's normal, especially for a kid's first time at day care, but I don't know... Now I keep asking myself, did she cry a lot when she first started staying with me? What if it's not normal and she's crying more there because the day care sucks?"

"Did the day care seem sucky to you?"

He shrugged again. "No, not really, but if they were going to act sucky, they wouldn't do it in front of people dropping off their kids and taking tours of the place, would they?"

"I bet you can look up the place online and find reviews from parents."

"Yeah, I thought of that. There weren't any horrible reviews. So maybe the place doesn't suck. But what if she just doesn't like it anyway?"

Maya tightened her hold on Arianna's leg, stepping on top of her foot and nearly causing her to stumble.

Arianna bent and pried her niece off of her leg, lifting her and holding her instead. "She might get used to it. But I get what you're saying – she's just a newborn. Way too young to ask whether she likes it there or not. You know…" She took a deep breath as she untangled one of Maya's fists from her hair, stopping her from pulling on it. "You don't have to leave her at a day care if you don't feel comfortable with that. You can always bring her here."

A knock came at the door, just as James looked about to reply.

"That must be my sister," Arianna said, stepping around him and opening the door after looking through the peep hole to confirm.

Selena's eyes widened when she saw James. Arianna didn't waste much time wondering what her sister thought of him being there. Moments later, after Arianna gave Maya a hug goodbye, both mother and daughter were gone.

"You ready to get out of here?" James asked.

"Sure. Just let me change into something date-worthy."

James looked her up and down, and she could feel his gaze lingering on her jeans and t-shirt, heating the skin beneath as if by magic. "I don't see anything wrong with what you're wearing."

"Well, my niece spit up mashed sweet potatoes on my sleeve, for one."

He shrugged. "I'm sure I've got baby puke somewhere on my clothes. If you do too, I won't feel like such a douche."

She laughed but ultimately retreated to her room to change, pulling on a v-neck blouse that was more flattering than her t-shirt had been, even without the spit-up vegetables.

When she returned to the living room, James was waiting.

"We'd better get going," he said as she grabbed her purse.

"Hungry?" she asked.

"Haven't given it much thought. It's just that it took all my willpower not to follow you back there to your bedroom. If we don't leave now…" His gaze sank to the deep V of cleavage her top exposed before he met her eyes.

For half a second, she considered sprinting back to her bedroom in faith that he'd follow.

In the end, willpower won out. A date would be fun, and it'd probably do James good to go out on the town sans-baby. For that matter, she needed to get out of her apartment, too.

They left in his car, and he offered to let her choose the restaurant. She opted to let him make the selection, since he'd chosen so well last time.

He drove them to a little corner place with brick pillars and large windows. Inside, the lighting cast a cozy-looking interior in warm shades of amber. The hostess was friendly and the scents drifting from the kitchen were just as appealing as the simple décor.

"This is really nice," she said, her memory drifting back to their first date, when they'd shared dinner and an incredible river view. "How do you find these places?" She was doubly glad she'd let him pick; his taste was impeccable.

He snorted. "Begging my co-workers for suggestions, mostly. If I was left to my own devices, we'd be ordering a couple of greasy cheesesteaks right about now. If you like the places we've gone to so far, you have Tyler and Jed to thank."

She wouldn't have minded greasy cheesesteaks, as long as it meant dinner in James' company. She kept that to herself though, picking up a menu and dragging her gaze away from him long enough to read it.

"So do you like to cook at home," she asked as she deliberated between chicken and pork tenderloin, "or do you just eat a lot of cheesesteaks?"

"I don't know if you can call it cooking, but I've figured out how to operate the stove in my apartment. Let's just say that most of the meals I come up with make the cold coffee and instant oatmeal you whipped up the other day look gourmet."

"About that." She laid down her menu. "I'm actually a decent cook, for the record. My mom taught me. And now I feel like I have to defend my own honor by making you dinner sometime."

"Well, you don't have to twist my arm. Just tell me when. And since I can count the number of real home-cooked meals I've eaten on one hand, I'm sure I'll be impressed no matter what."

"You'd better be, because I plan to pull out all the stops. And what do you mean you can count them on one hand? Didn't your parents cook?"

Some people just weren't into anything besides defrosting. Selena was like that, despite their mother's penchant for the culinary arts. Spending time in the kitchen had always been the one thing Arianna and her mother had really enjoyed doing together. Even after things had gotten rough between them, they'd made the occasional meal together. In silence, mostly, but still.

James shook his head. "My parents were always too stoned out of their minds to worry about things like food. My sister and I grew up in foster care. Most of the foster parents I was placed with had a bunch of kids and were more concerned with quantity than quality when it came to dinner."

Arianna's stomach knotted, taking the edge off her hunger as she absorbed what James had just said. Addict parents, and foster care? Looking into his eyes, she got the feeling that lackluster dinners hadn't been the worst of it. Suddenly, the way he'd gotten mad when she'd suggested he turn Emily over to the state made sense. Regret filled her as she realized she'd put a damper on their date by dredging up bad memories.

"Well then," she said, smiling and doing her best to gloss over her mistake, "I'm even more determined to cook for you now. Are there any foods you don't like? I don't want to spoil it with something you won't eat."

"I'll eat just about anything, but yeah – I'm not a big fan of chili."

"Really?" It was sort of a shame, because she had a great chili recipe. Still, there were plenty of other things she could make – some authentic Mexican cuisine, for instance. Her grandmother had passed down her method for making amazing homemade tortillas, plus dozens of her favorite recipes.

"Yeah. Years ago when Jed's wife died, he went through this phase where he taught himself to cook. Chili was the first thing he tried to master, and it was fucking awful. Like acidic meat juice that just about burnt a hole through your tongue. He made enough to feed an army every time, and since there were no armies around, he forced it on me and Tyler."

"Jed's wife died?" Arianna had met the owner of Hot Ink once, during her first visit to the studio, and had glimpsed him a couple times since then during her sessions with James. She'd never heard anything about him having a wife.

James nodded. "Years ago. He opened Hot Ink together with her, actually. He's engaged again now – getting married next month."

"Oh." Relief settled over Arianna, dispelling some of the sadness that had come with learning what Jed had gone through. "I'm glad to hear it." She could only imagine what it would be like to lose the person you'd sworn to spend forever with.

"Yeah. They're happy together, and he's a good guy – he deserves someone. I think everyone at Hot Ink is glad they're getting married."

The thought of the studio staff getting excited about Jed's new start made her smile. "It must be nice to have co-workers you're so close to, even if it means eating acid chili sometimes." Imagining James throwing his taste buds under the bus for the sake of his boss was funny and sort of sweet.

"Yeah, well, Tyler and I didn't have the heart to tell him how bad it was. Guess I was afraid that if we told him it was the shittiest thing to ever come off a stove burner, he'd give up and turn into a bachelor who survived off of TV dinners. After what he'd been through, that just seemed cruel."

Arianna nodded. "You did the right thing."

A server appeared and took their orders.

When he was gone, James shrugged. "Jed took me in for no good reason. I owed him. Eating his god-awful cooking was the least I could do."

"I'm sure he had a reason – you're amazingly talented. He had to see that."

"Talent doesn't mean much without training and practice. He taught me to tattoo and I'm sure there were times when I was a bigger pain in the ass than he'd bargained for."

It was hard to imagine James being a pain in the ass. He was the kindest and most hard-working person Arianna had ever met – the way he took care of Emily proved it, and his tattoos had the beauty and quality she'd normally expect to see in the work of an artist who'd been tattooing for years longer than he had.

Then again, people matured over time. Maybe he'd been different seven years ago.

She'd certainly made her share of mistakes when she'd been young.

"So," she said, changing the subject for her own sake as a familiar uneasiness threatened to set in, "what was the first thing you ever actually tattooed on someone?"

James smiled. "Well, Jed said he wouldn't unleash me on Hot Ink's clients until I was good enough that he'd be willing to let me tattoo him. So that's what he did. The design was—"

A phone went off, cutting James short. Arianna reached for her purse automatically before realizing that the ringtone wasn't hers.

James pulled his phone from a pocket. "Hello?"

For several seconds, he didn't say anything further. His expression darkened by degrees, until eventually he looked like a storm cloud was hanging over his head. Arianna almost wondered whether the caller had hung up on him, but he didn't put the phone down.

"Where the hell are you?" he asked, a sharpness to his voice Arianna had never heard before.

More silence, and then he swore.

Arianna's gut tied itself in knots that dulled her hunger. The easiness of their conversation had evaporated, and the amber lighting that filled the restaurant wasn't warm enough to erase the chill in his voice. Who could've upset him so severely with just a few words?

"Do you have any idea what kind of a risk you took by having some jackass just leave her on my doorstep? Anybody could've come along and taken her, hurt her. She was all alone when I found her. She was hungry, and she needed a diaper change. What the hell is wrong with you?"

Arianna felt the color drain out of her face. James' sister? A million questions raced through her mind, mostly ones that were similar to the ones he'd already asked.

"Yeah, well he didn't stay by her side," James said in response to something Arianna couldn't quite hear. "He left her on the doorstep and watched her from his car on the other side of the parking lot like a fucking coward."

A couple at the nearest table turned to stare.

James didn't seem to notice. Beneath his blond hair, his face was growing redder by the second. "Yeah, I read the note, and I've been taking care of her. She's doing fine, no thanks to you."

"What do you mean that was all you wanted to know – what about all the shit I want to know?"

A few more tense words were exchanged, during which James sat rigidly in his seat, his free hand curled in a white-knuckled fist. "90 days – I wonder if she'll even remember you by then. She was so small when you abandoned her."

He ended the call. Had he cut his sister off – had she tried to make excuses, or had his harsh words stunned her into silence?

They'd stunned Arianna into silence, and she'd only been an observer.

"That was my sister, Crystal." He finally met her eyes.

What she saw reflected there made her ache. Anger, yeah, but sadness too, and something she couldn't quite put her finger on. Regret, possibly. Or shame.

Or maybe she was just projecting the feelings lurking in the back of her mind onto him.

"I figured," she finally said.

"She's in some drug rehab program. Said she had to wait until the detox period was over to call."

"Some place nearby?" Arianna didn't know anything about drug rehab. She'd grown up in a conservative household, and drugs were part of a world she'd never waded into. She was the black sheep in the family, and she'd never touched anything so taboo.

"Near Philly. Guess that's where she's living now."

"And she called to ask about Emily?"

James nodded. "It would've served her right if I hadn't told her a damned thing. Acting like she cares after the way she just abandoned her…"

The tension in his jaw was visible, and a vein throbbed at his temple. "What kind of person would just leave their own kid? She wants to put on this concerned mother act, but if she'd ever given a shit about anyone but herself, she never would've abandoned Emily. Every kid deserves to be taken care of by their own parents, not pawned off on whoever will do the job."

James' words went straight through Arianna, causing sharp pain to flare in the vicinity of her heart while a creeping numbness radiated out into the rest of her. Her lips tingled, and though her hands rested on the table, she felt nothing – not the texture of the well-worn tabletop, or the coolness of the wood.

What kind of person would leave their own child to be raised by someone else?

Her. She would – she had.

James didn't know that, but it was easy to imagine that if he had, the same anger that rolled off him in waves now would be directed at her. Arianna didn't consider herself to be on the same base level as his sister – she certainly hadn't dumped her baby on a doorstep – but his words made it clear that he wouldn't see things the same way. And it was no wonder, considering the way he'd grown up: unwanted.

Regardless of how she'd done it, she'd surrendered her child to others to raise. And James obviously found that repellant.

Suddenly, she didn't feel like the girl in his tattoo chair anymore – the one he'd failed to disguise his lust for, the one he'd taken on a date. The one who'd seen and touched every last one of his tattoos, not to mention the hidden piercing that'd just about driven her out of her mind with pleasure. Instead, she felt like the girl she'd sacrificed so much trying not to be – a bad person. A bad mother.

Someone a selfless guy like James could never be attracted to.

Sitting there across from him as his date, she was living a lie. As soon as he found out about her past, he'd be out of her life quicker than she could blink.

The thought was heart-wrenching. She'd grown so attached to him, in such a short period of time. Emily, too. Maybe it'd be best to confess and leave – get it over with as quickly as possible, like tearing off a Band-Aid.

Maybe, but she couldn't bring herself to do it. Not while he was already seething, and not in public. It'd be devastating enough without an audience to see him look at her with the same disgust he obviously felt for his sister.

The waiter approached the table, oblivious to the tension that was so thick Arianna could've cut it with the knife that tumbled out of her napkin when she unwrapped her silverware.

The food that smelled so delicious tasted like ash in her mouth as she ate, mechanically carving bites from her plate as James did the same, chewing like he had a personal vendetta against his food.

"Sorry," he said, laying down his knife and fork with a clatter after he'd taken several bites. "I didn't mean to ruin our date."

She shook her head. "Don't worry about it." Things were ruined between them anyway; he just didn't know it yet.

"No, I mean it. This was supposed to be about you. I should be thinking about everything you've done, not everything Crystal failed to do."

"Really." She carved a bite of pork into too-small pieces. "I can't blame you for being upset. It's not like you knew she was going to call."

"I didn't even know she had my number. Figured she lost it ages ago."

Arianna nodded, toying with her fork. "So ... is she coming back? For Emily, I mean."

His frown deepened. "That's what she claims. The rehab thing she's doing is a 90 day program, and she says she's coming for Emily afterward."

That was two and a half months away. James didn't look pleased about it, though whether it was because he wanted Crystal to come sooner or not at all, it was hard to tell.

"She'd better be clean when she shows up," he said, glaring at nothing in particular, "because if she's going to touch drugs, she's not going to lay a finger on Emily."

It was obvious that he meant it. He looked so fiercely protective that Arianna's heart would've melted, if it hadn't been busy breaking.

"Forget about Crystal though," he said, shaking his head. "I can stop bitching about her if I really put my mind to it." He smoothed his expression with obvious effort, erasing lines from his brow. "We're on a date."

Arianna tried to smile. If her attempt was weak, he didn't complain.

"How was your day?" he asked.

His innocent question conjured up memories of Maya, driving Arianna's uneasiness even deeper. Not for the first time, she wondered how much Maya would resemble her own daughter when she was older – the cousin she'd never meet. The little girl Arianna had given birth to was 10 now – 10 years, 3 months and 16 days old, to be exact.

Sometimes Arianna wasn't sure what seemed more surreal: the fact that a decade had passed since she'd given birth, or the fact that it had happened at all. The experience had marked her more deeply than any other event ever had, yet at the same time, there were moments when she could hardly believe that she was really the same girl who'd brought a new life into the world and then left the hospital with empty arms.

"Okay," she said. "Tiring. I hate to tell you this, but babies are even more exhausting to take care of once they become mobile."

"I can't even imagine what it'd be like if Emily could run around on her own."

"Yeah, the running can be scary, especially if you're outside and have to worry about things like traffic and strange dogs. I took Maya to the park and she tried to tackle someone's yellow lab. The worst thing though is the climbing. She tried to scale the bookshelf in my bedroom and I about had a heart attack."

James' anger seemed to ebb as they made conversation, and by the time they finished their meals, his jaw had loosened and there was hardly a sign of the vein that'd been throbbing visibly earlier. When the waiter asked if they wanted dessert, he said yes.

They shared something dripping with chocolate and swimming in ice cream. The sweetness seemed foreign on Arianna's tongue, the vanilla strangely bitter. No matter how hard she tried, she just couldn't relax and enjoy it. Every two seconds or so, her imagination presented her with an image of James turning away in disgust when he learned she'd been a teen mother – a teen mother who'd chosen not to raise the child she'd given birth to.

Apparently, her distress didn't show. After paying the bill, James walked with her out of the restaurant, a hand against the small of her back. The light but sensual contact sent a shiver down her spine, allowing her to shrug off her sense of dread for just a second.

After that perfect moment ended, she savored the heat of his touch, fully aware that it might be the last time she ever felt it.

Except it wasn't. When they reached her apartment, he walked her to the door, then slipped inside, wrapping his arm around her waist so that the contact seemed natural, like anything else would've just been strange.

Even she had to admit to herself that it felt right, standing alone with him in her living room, the door locked behind them.

* * * * *

Arianna trembled lightly in James' arms. Feeling that – having tangible proof that she wanted this again, and just as badly as he did – had him painfully hard as he held her, breathing in the floral scent of her shampoo and faint cherry tang of her lip gloss. When he lowered his mouth over hers, the sweet flavor was crushed against his lips.

He'd hardly thought of anything else since they'd fucked the other evening – and night, and the following morning. The heat of her skin and texture of her bedsheets had been burnt into his memory, where he relived every heart-pounding, cock-stiffening moment of what they'd done. Several times hadn't been enough, even then, and the handful of days he'd gone without touching her since had left an ache deep in his balls.

All that was about to change. Pulse jumping in anticipation, he pulled her tight against him, letting the hard rod of his dick press against her belly.

She breathed sharply, a little moan leaving her lips only to be muffled by his.

The kiss went on, deepening until both of them were breathing harder than they had been at the start. When she shifted against him, leaning in and increasing the exquisite pressure her body put on his shaft, he broke the seal of their kiss.

"Fuck, I want you." The words tumbled out of his mouth, the truest thing he'd ever said.

Her eyes widened, and she shifted again, giving him a jolt that had his balls drawing closer to his already overheated body. She'd looked so beautiful during dinner; even when he'd been pissed over Crystal's phone call, he hadn't been able to stop admiring Arianna.

"I want you too," she said, staring up at him. At first it seemed like she was going to say more, but instead she shut her mouth, denting her lower lip as she bit it from the inside. One of her hands drifted over his hip and she loosened her embrace a little.

Her fingertips were only an inch or two away from the hardness straining the front of his jeans. Slipping his hand over hers, he guided her touch there, unable to resist.

Her hand felt like heaven against his dick, even through his jeans. As she rubbed the underside of his shaft, his mind filled with visions of her beneath him, breasts rising and falling as he drove himself into her.

Or on top of him. He'd take her any way he could get her, and love it.

"Should we go to the bed, or see just how much that table will hold up to after all?" He ran a hand over the contours of her side, letting it dip into the hourglass notch below her ribs and come to rest on her hip.

Another one of those shivers went through her – he was so close he felt it easily, and it made his skin prickle with desire. Had she been thinking about last time as often and as hard as he had?

Hopefully. Probably, judging by the way she shook against him.

"Bed," she finally said, her grip tightening around his erection.

He groaned, so ready to feel her pussy wrenching tight and hot around his shaft that he could hardly stand it.

He didn't waste any time heading exactly where she'd said, taking her by the hand as they hurried toward her room.

She was like hot silk in his hands – warm and pliant, a pleasure to feel under his fingertips no matter how or where he touched her. He undressed her as quickly as he could while still taking the time to admire her body, his hands tracing and cupping her curves.

When he'd uncovered and touched every inch of her – hands lingering on the places that made her draw sharp breaths – he stopped exploring her body long enough to strip his own bare.

Or at least, he managed to pull off his shirt. That was as far as he got before he felt her hands at his waist, fingertips slipping beneath the waistband of his jeans as she worked the button through its hole.

His hard-on fell right into her hand when she unzipped his fly. Before he knew it she'd pulled down his underwear too, letting her fingers curl around his shaft as she formed a fist.

A tight fist that had his blood roaring in his ears as she slid it up and down, the edge of her palm kissing the head of his dick at the end of each stroke. It felt good. Not as good as being buried balls-deep in her pussy, but still – good enough that he forgot about everything else, his world narrowing to include nothing but her and him and the effects of her touch.

That world shattered when she lowered her head into his lap, redefining what pleasure was with the simple act of touching the tip of her tongue to the underside of his cock. She traced the length of his shaft that way, her breath ghosting over his skin, heating it even more than the blood rushing beneath the surface already had.

He looked down, watching her upper lip brush his hard flesh as her tongue peeked pink and wet from beneath. It wasn't a surprise to see a drop of come shining pearl-white at the slit bisecting the head of his dick.

It *was* a surprise when she licked it away, tongue tracing that tiny notch before her lips closed around him. The shock of heat and pressure tore deep into him, freeing a moan that started out wordless and ended in her name.

She took him deeper, lips sliding down his shaft as her tongue caressed it from beneath, creating smooth friction that made his balls ache.

She didn't take him all the way in, though she came close, her lip coming within a bare inch of the captive bead at the base of his cock. When she slid a hand up his thigh and over his fallen jeans, cupping his balls, it was all he could do not to come in her mouth.

He slid a hand over the curve of her skull, letting his fingers get tangled in her locks as he resisted the urge to pull them, guiding her to go farther and harder. "I'm going to come," he said, "if you don't stop now."

She slid back, running her tongue down the underside of his shaft 'till the last moment, when he popped free of her mouth altogether. Her eyes flickered up to his. "You don't want me to stop then, do you?"

He was painfully hard, his skin stretched taut and wet from being inside her mouth. She still held his balls in her hand, too. It was easy to imagine her parting her lips and sliding back down on him, sucking him off to completion. "Guess that's up to you."

It wasn't like that'd be the end of things. Her pussy was a temptation he wouldn't be able to resist in any case; coming this way wouldn't be enough to make his dick go soft. He had her all to himself, for once – they had time to take their time, within reason.

She rose higher, still kneeling, and pressed her lips to his.

They were hot, wet and the tiniest bit salty. He thrust his tongue between them, kissing her hard as he palmed one of her breasts, feeling her nipple go stiff against his fingers.

He didn't stop her when she rocked back. Seconds later she had him in her mouth again, driving him crazy with her tongue and lips, her fingertips brushing the sensitive skin behind his balls. Her hair spilled across his thighs, lying dark against his jeans and the exposed skin above.

He came hard, reveling in the pressure her mouth exerted on the head of his dick as come rushed out of him and over her tongue. A small sound rose up from somewhere in her throat and spurred him on, adding another layer to his pleasure. Taking him deeper, she tightened her grip on his balls, rolling them against her palm. The bliss might've blinded him if he hadn't had his eyes tightly shut. He couldn't focus on anything else, not even the way she looked as she swallowed, her mouth tightening around his cock.

She kept her mouth on his dick until he pulled free, finally using his hold on her hair to guide her – away and out of his lap, where he could see her face.

Her lips were red and a little puffy, eyes bright. The golden flecks in her irises shone, flickering when she exhaled and blinked.

"That felt so damn good."

Understatement of the century. If he could've gone back and relived the last minute of what she'd just done to him, he would've, over and over again until it killed him. There was just nothing else he'd rather do, ever, if given the choice. Except for maybe pushing her thighs wide apart and driving his still-stiff dick between them, fucking her until she made sounds of pleasure a lot louder than the one she'd made when he'd exploded in her mouth.

Color burnt bright pink across her cheekbones. Was she really blushing or was that just the natural effect of blood rushing to the surface of the skin, summoned there by arousal, by touching and being touched?

Unlike him, she was fully naked. He took advantage of that fact, slipping a hand between her legs and stroking the silky-soft lips of her pussy, testing for wetness.

He found it in spades; his fingertips slipped against her slick skin, and when he pulled them away, they shone.

She'd more or less melted against him when he'd touched her like that, a fact that eliminated the little bit of softness that'd set in after his orgasm. Growing harder by the second, he kicked his jeans and underwear all the way off, then pressed her down onto the bed, using his body to guide hers down.

She was so soft against him, so warm. Except for her nipples; those were hard as glass. He teased one with his fingertips, drawing the other into his mouth as he lay stretched beside her.

Arching against the mattress, she sighed, pressing her breast more firmly against his face. The soft flesh radiated heat that he could feel building up inside him too, readying his body for another climax. Still, ready or not, he'd thought of a good reason to defer.

Biting her nipple lightly before raising his head from her chest, he slid down the bed, down her body, settling between her legs and kneeling there.

Her pussy glistened. He added to that natural wetness when he pressed his open mouth against her flesh, tonguing the hard little bud her clit had become.

Her hips bucked against his face and his tongue slipped, delving into her entrance, into heat and pressure he couldn't help imagining wrapped around his dick. The thought drove him as he lashed his tongue against her soft skin, aching to feel and hear her come.

In the peripheral field of his vision, he saw her hands clasp shut, forming fists around sections of rumpled sheet. Holding on hard to the bedclothes like that, she gasped.

It was a unique sound, both ragged and soft somehow. He knew what it meant, knew just what to do to cause her to make it again. Pressing a finger into her, he ran the tip up and down her inner wall, fucking her that way as he sucked her clit.

It worked. She writhed, grasping the sheet harder than ever, pulling on it as she gasped, again and again. The sound became a part of her breathing, a soundtrack that marked each second of her climax as he did everything he could to make it last.

His face was as wet as her pussy when he finally stopped, rising and grabbing his jeans, pulling a condom from a pocket and ripping open the package as quickly as he could. His fingers slipped and slid down the sides of his dick as he sheathed himself, so desperate to be inside her it hurt.

Moments later, he had his wish, and her pussy was wrenching tight around his shaft. Whether she was doing it on purpose or the tightening was involuntary, it felt mind-blowingly good. Not even having his dick sucked had felt as good as the sheer, simple pleasure of having her on her back beneath him. On top of her, he was on top of the world, lost in how perfect everything felt as she wrapped her legs around his waist.

She arched, just like she had when he'd eaten her pussy. This time, her body's natural reaction pressed her breasts against his chest, rubbing her nipples against his skin. He could've come then and there, but he held out, fucking her steadily instead of giving in and finishing in a burst of frenzied pleasure.

Waiting got him exactly what he'd wanted: another gasp from her, another climax that made her pussy shrink fast and hard around his thrusting dick. The pressure was exquisite, and so was the sound of his name on her lips. He could've listened to that forever, but soon she was breathless, relapsing into silence as her orgasm faded and she unwrapped her legs from around him, like she'd couldn't keep them up anymore.

That was it; he couldn't wait any longer. If she wanted more after he came, he'd give it to her however she wanted – with his mouth or hands, with his cock, if she wanted, after it got hard again. Even now, he had a feeling that wouldn't take long. Fuck, she drove him crazy. When she was beneath him, he didn't know when to quit.

Sharp little bursts of pain heated his skin when she raked her nails down his back, then gripped his ass cheeks. Her nails settled into the cleft above his thighs as she clung to him, urging him to go harder.

He did exactly that, groaning as gratification crashed down on him, pulling him under the surface of another orgasm. Last time had felt good, but this was something different – and even better – altogether. They were chest-to-chest and hip-to-hip, bodies tangled together. Even their breath mingled as she gasped. Pleasure swept through him, white-hot, and it was like being struck by lightning: a few seconds of mounting sensation that erupted into something blindingly powerful and then left him feeling stricken, still charged with something he was in awe of.

When he pulled out, her nails raked his skin again, biting as she gave up her embrace, seemingly reluctant.

He knew the feeling; he didn't really want to give up the mind-blowing closeness they'd found, either. Settling so close beside her that his cock rested against her hip, he laid a hand on one of her breasts.

She turned into him, her breath rushing across his lips.

It was an invitation he couldn't resist. Covering her mouth with his, he relaxed into a kiss that put a seal on what they'd just done, committing it to a place in his memory he knew he'd revisit again and again.

Time stretched on after the kiss ended, and when she eventually stirred against him, slinging an arm over his side, he was halfway asleep.

He was so comfortable lying there with her draped halfway across him, leaving was the last thing he wanted to do. Moving was second to last. "I've got to head to Jed and Karen's to pick up Emily," he forced himself to say.

She nodded, her disheveled hair rippling against his shoulder. "Wish you didn't have to go."

She sounded like she meant it, and that made him happy and unhappy at the same time. She deserved more time, more devotion, from anyone lucky enough to wind up in her bed. He couldn't give it to her though. Rising, he got dressed and left her alone, still naked and so beautiful it killed a part of him to leave her.

"Wish I didn't have to go either," he said, and did just that.

* * * * *

She heard him lock the door from the inside before he left. That should've pleased her, but safety aside, she hated the idea of a locked door between them.

Lying still where he'd left her, with the sheets still dented at her side where he'd been, she held onto the last moments of fading pleasure. For now, she still tingled where he'd touched her, still felt the heat of his body against hers. And she wanted those moments to last, because she knew she wouldn't be reliving them in the future.

She felt guilty for staying silent and surrendering to the chemistry between them, but only a little. They'd both had a good time; she doubted he'd regret it much when she finally did tell him about her past, since they'd already done it several times before. What difference would one more incredible time make, in the long run?

She was going to lose him either way.

CHAPTER 10

11 Years Ago

It'd taken Arianna days to work up the courage to tell her mom that she was pregnant. She'd meant to do it as soon as she'd gotten home from school that day, but now it was going on six and her dad was due home from work in a few minutes. Time was running out.

"Mom, I have to tell you something." Arianna's pulse throbbed in her temples, giving her a headache as she cut a red pepper into thin slivers for the salad that would accompany the spaghetti she'd just finished preparing meatballs for.

"What is it?"

Arianna's throat constricted, silencing her with a choking sensation. She fought to work past it, to speak. She had to tell her mom before her dad got home, because as agonizing as confessing at all was, telling her mother first would be the easiest option. If she told them both at the same time, they'd be able to team up against her. This way...

"What did you want to tell me?" her mother asked, stirring the pan of sauce and meat that simmered on the stove.

Arianna worked her stiff tongue loose, ignoring her dry mouth. "I'm pregnant."

Her mother dropped the wooden spoon into the sauce pan, then turned a few seconds later, as if shock had delayed her reaction. "Are you sure?"

Arianna resisted the urge to shrink beneath her gaze. "Yeah."

Her mother's pale blue eyes grew wide, and little lines appeared around her mouth as it shrank into a thin line. "Are you and Cody having sex?" She spat out the question like she was accusing Arianna of an act of international terrorism.

"We were," Arianna said, resisting the urge to add 'obviously'. Every last fiber of her being was on edge, trying and failing to harden her heart in self-defense. She could imagine seeing the same angry look in her father's eyes, knew she'd see it as soon as he got home and found out.

Her mother sucked in a breath, then hissed out Arianna's name. "I knew we shouldn't have let you spend so much time with that boy. I told your father…"

The sauce bubbled around the fallen spoon, but Arianna's mother didn't pay any attention. "How far along are you?" Her gaze zeroed in on Arianna's mid-section, and a pang of agony sailed through her as she remembered Cody eyeing her the same way just days ago.

He hadn't snapped out of his selfish stupor, hadn't so much as held her hand since then. In fact, he'd only spoken to her twice, both times to urge her to choose an abortion.

"I don't know."

"Well, how long ago did you…"

Arianna clamped her mouth shut, tasting blood as she clipped the tip of her tongue. Every one of her mother's questions felt like a red-hot needle, prodding deep and reminding her of Cody's rejection.

"What are we going to do? Arianna, you're only a sophomore in highschool. What were you thinking?"

Arianna didn't say anything, didn't admit that she hadn't been thinking at all, she'd been feeling. Feeling like the center of someone's universe for the first time in her life, feeling like there was someone who understood her, who wouldn't want to exist without her. Of course, now she saw all that for the illusion it was. She didn't need her mother waving a sauce-stained spoon to remind her that it'd all blown up in her face, to make her feel stupid.

The searing pain that'd burnt its way into every fiber of her being did a good enough job on its own.

"Your father is going to be furious." Her mother exhaled, loudly and slowly. "You're not even halfway finished with highschool! You still have two and a half more years to go, not to mention college..."

Everything inside Arianna seemed to shrivel up. She resisted the urge to let her fingertips drift over her belly, to try to detect the unseen presence that was driving everyone away from her, creating distance that only harsh words could cross. Funny thing was, she couldn't feel the baby at all. Not yet. But she felt everything else, felt everything crumbling around her. It would've been surreal, if it hadn't been so devastating.

"You can't undo a mistake like this," her mother said, as if Arianna was incapable of grasping the gravity of her situation. "Why couldn't you have just waited?"

Arianna said nothing. It wasn't like she'd been blindsided by her mother's reaction. Unlike when she'd confessed to Cody, she hadn't been expecting anything like understanding. Problem was, she'd counted on having his support, at least, when she'd faced everyone else. Her and him against the world, only now...

It was just her, and without anyone to share her burden, the world was vast and dark. Love would've been a buffer against the harshness – other people's judgments wouldn't have mattered much if she'd had just one person to stand by her side. But love was something she'd gambled for and lost – she realized now that she'd never had it. Two blue lines had revealed her future to be one epic problem, and love wasn't part of the equation.

* * * * *

"Wow," Karen said, standing outside James' booth with her hands on her hips. "She was cute. And I'm pretty sure she would've sold her soul for a date with you. Don't you like brunettes?"

James turned away, putting his back to Karen and the dark-haired woman who'd just left his booth. "Uh, it wasn't that." Did he like brunettes?

Hell yes, he liked brunettes. But he'd hardly noticed the woman's hair color, let alone anything else about her. Thoughts of his time alone with Arianna two days ago were still whirling through his mind, blinding him to distractions like the girl who'd just dropped half a dozen not-so-subtle hints concerning him – or certain parts of him, anyway.

He'd pierced the cartilage of her left ear. Then he'd given her care instructions, and hadn't bothered to watch her leave. That was it.

"What was it then?" Karen leaned on the wall. "Are things going okay with your niece?"

"Yeah, they're going all right. It's just that I'm seeing someone."

He turned around in time to see Karen's auburn eyebrows fly up to her hairline. "Really? Who is she?"

She braced her chin on her palm, like she was settling in to hear a particularly juicy story.

"I met her here. Tattooed her several times."

"How long have you been going out?"

"Just a couple weeks. Since she was a client, I didn't want to freak her out by asking too soon, you know?"

Karen nodded. "So... Are things serious?"

James turned back to his booth, straightening a piece of art hanging on the wall – not that it needed it. "Haven't been seeing each other that long."

The half-answer felt uncomfortably like a lie. It was true that they'd only been going out for a matter of weeks, but he'd never felt more serious about anyone. Whether that was due more to his lack of meaningful relationships or more to the deep-seated attraction he felt for Arianna, it didn't matter – he knew how he felt. What he had with Arianna was more than a fling.

In fact, the thought of them drifting amicably apart after a few nights together – or stolen afternoon hours – made him feel vaguely sick. The more of her he got, the more he wanted. And he knew in his bones that no matter how many fish there were in the sea, there were none that could replace her.

"Well, I was sure Jed was the one right away, on our first date," Karen said. "Before then, actually, if I'm being totally honest. Sometimes you just know."

A couple weeks ago, James would've thought that was bullshit – though he never would've said that out loud to Karen. Now, it didn't seem so stupid.

"Sorry if I'm being nosy." Karen straightened to her full height. "It's just that I was thinking you might like to bring a date to the wedding. You're allowed a plus one, you know. So if you really like this girl… This is a prime opportunity to impress her with how handsome you'll look in your tux. Just saying."

"Yeah. I really like her."

When he turned around again, Karen was grinning. "Great. I'll put you down for two then."

James didn't argue. Truth was, he did 'just know' – knew that Arianna walking through the doors of Hot Ink was the best thing that'd happened to him since he'd walked through those same doors seven years ago.

* * * * *

Arianna reached under her bed and pulled out a heart-shaped box – a remnant of some long-ago Valentine's Day. Her parents had given her the chocolates when she'd still been in high school; they'd done that for her and Selena every February 14th throughout their childhoods. It had been a sweet tradition, one that pre-dated the trouble that'd put a rift between her and her parents; maybe that was why she'd chosen the box to store some of her most treasured possessions in.

Her heart skipped a beat as she lifted the lid, just like it always did. She knew exactly how many photos were inside, all but one wrapped in lined paper bearing neat handwriting.

She kept the pictures carefully organized. The one on top had been taken inside a hospital, just minutes after she'd given birth. In it, she held her daughter close to her chest, wrapped in a receiving blanket. It was the only one of the photos that had been taken with her camera.

The second photo was wrapped in the letter it had come with, a piece of mail that had been postmarked on her baby's first birthday. The rest had been sent the same way; every year, the couple who'd adopted Arianna's child sent an update letter and new photo on her birthday.

Every once in a while, Arianna reread the ten letters she'd collected so far. And she always read new ones on the day they arrived. That was as far as she'd taken the openness of the adoption.

It wasn't that she didn't care, or that she felt intimidated by the family who was raising her baby. On the contrary; she'd chosen the couple herself and they'd been a bright spot in the otherwise confusing and lonely period of her pregnancy. They'd been so kind and understanding – in ways her family often hadn't been – and that was what had reinforced her decision to choose adoption.

They'd flown in from Connecticut during the last trimester of Arianna's pregnancy just to meet with her, and talking to them had been a relief. Her parents had been all for the adoption – actually, they'd suggested it first, almost as soon as she'd confessed her condition – but they'd still treated her pregnancy as something shameful. An epic mistake that she'd felt hanging over her head like a black cloud any time her mother or father had so much as glanced at her.

As soon as her pregnancy had started to show, everyone – her family included – had looked at her differently. It'd been like she wasn't even a person anymore, just a walking disappointment for family and strangers alike to heap their judgment on.

Joy and Dave, on the other hand, had talked about her pregnancy like it was some sort of gift. The contrast had been so stark that Arianna had started shedding tears of relief about five minutes into their first conversation. It was then that she'd realized she definitely wanted them to be her daughter's parents. She'd even invited Joy to be present for the birth.

They'd told her she'd be welcome to come see them in Connecticut, if she ever wanted to. While Arianna had appreciated it, she'd never gone. Her daughter was their daughter, now; it would simply hurt too much to visit. Knowing she was healthy and happy was enough ... or at least as close to enough as it could get.

Fact was, even ten years later, having given up her baby still hurt. It always would, even if she knew her daughter was much better off with Joy and Dave... It would always hurt because she loved her, and it was hard to love someone so much and have so many years and miles between herself and them. Not a day went by that she didn't think of her.

Still, some days were worse than others, and this was definitely one of those days. Maybe it was because she'd spent nearly two weeks caring for Emily only to have that situation ended abruptly, but she felt the loss more acutely than she had at any time since her daughter's last birthday.

As stinging pressure mounted behind her eyes, she picked up the first picture and traced the contour of her newborn daughter's tiny cheek.

From somewhere in the distance, her phone rang.

After laying down the picture, it took her a minute to remember where she'd left her phone. By the time she found it on the kitchen counter, it was on its fourth ring. She barely glanced at the screen before answering, and the name there was blurred by unshed tears. "Hello?"

She did her best to keep her voice steady, in case it was one of her clients – maybe the start-up tech firm she was currently designing a logo for.

"Arianna."

Those three syllables, spoken in a voice that made her heart beat faster even in the midst of freshly-rekindled grief, dispelled all notions of the man on the other end of the connection being a client.

"James."

A second or two of silence slipped by, and she used the opportunity to wipe the moisture from her eyes with the back of her hand.

"Yeah, it's me," he said, as if there could be any doubt. "How are things?"

"Quiet," she said. "Really quiet, without Emily or my niece here. I got a lot of work done today." At the moment, she couldn't have cared less about that, but pretending that she did beat telling James she'd almost been in tears over a box of photos.

"That's good. Listen… Remember how I told you my boss Jed is getting married in a couple weeks?"

"Yes."

"Well, I'm allowed to bring someone to the wedding. A date. Would you like to come with me?"

His question sliced through her, inciting a split second of excitement and decimating it just as quickly. A couple days ago, she would've been delighted if he'd asked her to go as his date to his boss' wedding. That was before he'd heard from his sister – before Arianna had realized that he'd never want to be with a woman who'd given up her own child, for any reason.

She couldn't blame him. Not really, in light of how he'd grown up and what his sister had put him through now, as an adult. But understanding why he felt the way he did didn't make it any less painful for her. She liked him so much ... and wanted so badly to be someone he could like back.

But that just wasn't going to happen. She'd faced hard realities before, and steeled herself to do so again now.

"I don't think that's a good idea," she forced herself to say, fully aware that there was no way she could keep her secret over the coming weeks. Feeling like she was hiding something from him for just the past couple days had been utterly exhausting. Besides, she didn't *want* to have secrets. If she was ever going to really fall in love, it had to be with someone who could love her – the real her – back.

"You don't?"

She'd spent so much time dwelling on his voice – replaying things he'd said to her inside her head – that she could detect traces of surprise and even pain in his tone. He wasn't one to wear his heart on his sleeve, but over the course of just a couple weeks, she'd gotten to know him well enough to know that she'd hurt him.

"No. James... I've really enjoyed these past couple weeks." Pressure built up behind her eyes again, but she absolutely refused to give in to it. "But I can't go with you to the wedding, because I don't think what we have is made to last much longer. We're just not compatible enough ... you'll be tired of me by the time your boss gets married, I'm sure."

He was quiet for so long that she actually thought he might've hung up. Her heart plunged, then leapt painfully back into place when the sound of his voice came from the other end of the connection.

"Tired of you? Do you really think that?"

"Yes." Maybe 'disgusted by' would've been a more accurate choice of words, but the gist was the same, and she'd decided to keep her secret just that – secret.

She just couldn't deal with the judgmental looks, the passive-aggressive disgust that would reveal itself in barbed questions and exclamations of disbelief. Not from James. As a pregnant teen, she'd heard it all from her own family, and even now, a decade later, she wasn't ready to relive it all again. It was simple, really: she liked and respected him too much to bear his judgment. It would crush her.

At least this way, she wouldn't have those excruciating memories to spoil the amazing ones he'd given her. And he wouldn't have to bear the burden of knowing he'd been involved with someone with a past like hers. It was better this way, for both of them.

"You don't know a damn thing about me if you think I'm going to be tired of you in a couple weeks," he said.

The pressure behind her eyes increased, becoming painful. "Maybe you're right – maybe we don't know that much about each other. Which is why you're bound to be disappointed if things go any further. I'm sorry, but you're just going to have to trust me. There's no way this can work."

"Did I do something? Say something to piss you off? Because—"

"No. You didn't do or say anything to make me mad. Really." He'd treated her wonderfully, but that was because he didn't know the truth about her.

"Okay. So you're just tired of me already. I got it." His voice rang with disappointment and resignation.

An ache spread through the center of Arianna's chest, right over her heart. "No. It's not that." She bit her tongue before she could say something cliché like 'it's not you, it's me'.

"It's all right, Arianna. I always knew you were out of my league."

He hung up before she could say another word.

She couldn't have spoken anyway, even though he had it all backwards. Her throat had constricted and the tears she'd been working so hard to hold back had finally begun to slip free, one by one. She'd never be free of the choices she'd made when she'd been just 16; even now the consequences radiated throughout her life, causing pain.

For the second time in her life, she'd given up someone she loved for the sake of what was best. It was a miserable feeling, no matter how much sense it made, and something told her that years from now she'd still be thinking of this loss, just like she still thought of the first one.

* * * * *

"Hey James." Jed stood outside James' booth, taking up the entire aisle that ran down the center of Hot Ink. "Karen wants to know if your date will want steak or salmon at the reception."

James tensed as he finished readjusting his tattoo chair, which had accommodated a client just five minutes ago. "Don't worry about it; I'm not bringing anyone."

Jed's eyebrows crept together, lining his forehead. "Karen said you were going to bring a woman you'd been seeing. She said you met her here."

"We're not seeing each other anymore." Saying it out loud was a bitch. As he spoke, dual waves of frustration and shame crept over him, underlaid by deep disappointment. He would've felt stupid admitting it now, but he'd been completely caught off guard when Arianna had told him she didn't want to see him anymore.

The more he thought about her and what she'd said, the more he felt like a jackass for being shocked. Not only was Arianna the sexiest woman he'd ever seen, she was smart and educated, selfless and self-sufficient. A woman like that was out of virtually any guy's league, let alone his. She could have anyone, so what exactly did he have to offer her in the long run?

The sex they'd had had been unbelievably fucking hot. He knew she'd loved it; he wasn't stupid or self-depreciating enough to pretend otherwise. But obviously, she wanted something more than that – something she didn't think he could give her.

"That's too bad." Jed just stood there, and James felt the other man's gaze boring into him.

"Sorry if I fucked up your guest count, or whatever."

"Not a big deal. All this planning is last-minute, anyway. You sure you don't wanna bring anyone?"

"Yeah." He turned his back to Jed, messing around with supplies inside his booth as a thinly-veiled invitation for Jed to leave him alone.

No such luck.

"Karen seemed to think you two were pretty serious. Why the sudden change?"

James swallowed a knot of frustration, willing the tension out of his muscles. "We weren't as serious as I thought. Judgment error, that's all."

"Maybe it's none of my business, but whatever you had with this girl started here in my shop, so I'm gonna butt in anyway. After Karen and I first got together, there was a time when I thought she wasn't interested in me anymore. Figured she'd gotten tired of me, and how could I blame her? She could have anyone she wanted."

James heard what Jed was saying, but didn't dare let it resurrect any sort of hope inside him. Not everyone was as lucky as Jed and Karen.

"I was wrong," Jed said. "And when I realized that, I felt pretty damn stupid. So before you write whatever you had with this girl off as a lost cause, you need to make sure you're not just being stupid."

James met Jed's eyes. "Did Karen ever tell you that you two just weren't compatible? That what you had – everything you'd thought had been going so great – wasn't cut out to last?"

Jed's silence said it all – Karen had never said anything like that to him. Which was no surprise; anyone who'd ever seen them together could see that she loved him.

"Shit. Sorry."

He left James alone, just like he'd wanted. It wasn't exactly the relief he'd thought it would be.

In less than five minutes, he was back. "You wanna go out for a drink tonight?"

James shook his head. "Can't. Have to take care of Emily." Having a baby basically meant that he couldn't go anywhere or do anything that wasn't baby-friendly, and a bar definitely wasn't that.

"Karen will be glad to watch her while we go out for a while – I just called and asked her. She has a shoot she'll be wrapping up around seven, and then she'll be free."

"I don't wanna take advantage—"

"You're not sitting at home alone with that baby and being miserable. We'll let Tyler close up tonight, and you and I will head out after your last appointment."

* * * * *

Arianna tapped away on her keyboard, ignoring the Photoshop icon at the bottom of her screen, where the program was hidden away. She'd planned to wrap up work on her logo design, give it a last going-over before presenting the final product to her client tomorrow. Instead, she ignored her job, focusing on her internet browser instead. Selena had just picked up Maya, and after a full day of babysitting the little girl, Arianna was physically and emotionally exhausted.

For the first time in nearly a year, she logged onto the online birthmother support forum she'd first started using as a teenager. Online conversation wasn't a perfect substitute for real human interaction, but she had a surplus of people in real life who could never understand what she'd gone through, and she was at her limit.

For nearly an hour, she scrolled through the forum, reading others' threads, soothed a little by the reminder that she wasn't alone in her experiences or feelings, even if it felt like it. Eventually, she worked up the courage to stop lurking and post a thread of her own.

After typing and deleting a subject line several times, she finally settled on: *'Dating as a first mom – is it possible to find someone who understands?'*

In the body of her post, she briefly shared that she'd ended a relationship with someone she'd really liked because he couldn't have accepted the decision she'd made to give her daughter a life with an adoptive family.

Replies started coming in within minutes. Some of them were supportive, written by women who reported finding understanding significant others. Some of them were in happy dating relationships, and others were married. Some even had children with their boyfriends or husbands now. Those replies offered the hope Arianna had sought, though right now she couldn't think past James to imagine another man entering her life.

Other replies were more along the lines of commiseration. It seemed like a lot of women had dated men who'd said hurtful things, or even put them down for choosing to place their babies with adoptive families.

'If he can't accept that your decision was a sacrifice, not an easy way out, then you deserve better,' read one user's reply.

'I dated a guy just like him once,' said another. *'I hoped he'd come around eventually, but he never did. I always felt judged by him, and eventually I got tired of it. I wanted to have a family someday, but even though he claimed we were serious, every time I brought it up he'd blow me off, like he couldn't believe I'd want to have another baby. Breaking it off with him was one of the smartest decisions I ever made. You've been through enough pain – don't stay with someone who's only going to hurt you.'*

Other replies were more blunt. *'Forget about him. You deserve a real man, not a selfish jerk who can't wrap his head around the fact that placing a baby with adoptive parents isn't an easy way out. If he broke up with you after he found out about your baby, he doesn't deserve you.'*

Arianna's heart sank as she read the last reply, and her fingers tingled with the urge to type back, to defend James. Somehow, she'd messed even this up – hadn't been clear enough. He wasn't a selfish jerk. He was anything but.

'I'm the one who ended things, not him,' she wrote. *'I think my original post was misleading. He's a wonderful guy, but I knew he wouldn't be able to understand why I placed my daughter for adoption because of some things he's endured in his personal life, and I felt like I couldn't stand to face his disappointment.'*

She forced herself to work on the logo for several minutes, then brought up her browser and refreshed the page.

The other user had written back. *'If he's so wonderful, why didn't you tell him and at least give him a chance? You never know – his reaction might surprise you.'*

The other woman's reply cut Arianna to the quick, inciting a bout of guilt and second-guessing. At the same time, she couldn't help but think of the way James had been saddled with his niece, and the years he'd spent in foster care. He hadn't gone into much detail, but he obviously hadn't had a happy childhood.

The words he'd spoken on their second date echoed inside her head, playing on a loop: *"What kind of person would just leave their own kid? Every kid deserves to be taken care of by their own parents, not pawned off on whoever will do the job."*

Quickly, she typed *'I'm not that brave,'* and closed the browser.

It was the sad truth.

CHAPTER 11

"It's a damn good thing you're getting married," James said. "If anyone needs a ring on their finger, it's you."

The bar was crowded with both men and women, but most of the females seemed to have eyes only for Jed. Maybe it was the fact that he radiated indifference that drove them so crazy; with his stoic expression and knack for speaking in one or two word sentences, he gave 'hard to get' a whole new meaning.

Or maybe it was the fact that his massive size and tapestry of tattoos made him stand out so severely. If the women at the end of the bar stared at him any harder, their overly made-up eyes were likely to pop right out of their skulls.

Jed made a wordless sound that was something like a grunt, then took a long sip of his beer. "Don't know what you're talking about."

"Like hell you don't. The bartender keeps polishing your section of the bar every two seconds just to be near you, even though it's clean. If you actually spilled your drink, I'm pretty sure she'd die from the thrill of it."

Jed shrugged, his huge shoulders straining his t-shirt, much to the observing ladies' delight. "Maybe it's you she's after. Ever think of that?"

James shook his head as he took a sip of his own beer, barely tasting the lager. "Nah. It's you. Does Karen have any idea what it's like when you go out to places like this without her?" He couldn't help but wonder if Karen would've been so eager to babysit Emily if she'd realized.

"Typical," was all Jed said.

"What's typical?"

"You underestimating yourself, thinking you're not good enough."

"What the hell are you talking about?"

"I just saw a girl almost put her eye out with the tiny umbrella in her drink because she was staring at you," Jed said.

"I don't give a shit, even if it's true. I hope you didn't bring me out here just to try to hook me up with some chick from a bar." Right now, he was incapable of even trying to work up any enthusiasm for a fling. He was still hurting from the last time he'd done that, with a beautiful woman he'd tattooed...

Yeah, he was still reeling from her rejection and was forced to admit to himself that she'd come closer to breaking his heart than anyone else ever had. Hell, maybe she *had* broken it. All he knew was that there was a pain right below his breastbone that intensified whenever he thought of her.

"I didn't," Jed said. "Karen would kill me – now that she's got the idea of you dating into her head, she's determined that you need a happily ever after. You're the only single person left at Hot Ink."

James snorted. He'd probably be Hot Ink's most eligible bachelor for a long time. Forever, if his inability to give a damn about any woman who wasn't Arianna persisted.

"What I'm trying to do," Jed continued, "is make you see that you have a bad habit of putting yourself down. You've gotten better over the past few years, but I can still see it. You think you're not good enough for that woman you were seeing, don't you?"

"I'm *not*."

"Yes you are. I asked you to be my best man because I respect the hell out of you. Stop thinking you're shit just because things didn't work out between you and your girlfriend. It pisses me off to see you doing it. There are a lot of other women out there who'd be glad to date you, and you know it."

Yeah, 'date'. He'd 'dated' more than a few women in the past, usually for a night at a time. Sometimes longer, but he'd never gotten anywhere near the level of seriousness he'd felt with Arianna. And he'd been okay with that, until he'd had a taste of her. Now the idea of going back to having flings with women he only liked and could never love seemed lame.

He said something like that to Jed, who nodded. "If you think this woman is that special, maybe you should give it one more shot. And if that doesn't work out, give yourself some time to get over it, but don't go beating yourself up."

James didn't say anything. He respected Jed, but what Arianna had said had been pretty damn clear.

A couple of women materialized beside Jed, cosmos in hand. One was dressed in a sparkly t-shirt and the other had hair so huge it dominated her appearance, rendering her clothing utterly forgettable. They both wore big grins.

Jed took a long drink from his beer and replied with a simple "hey" when they tossed out greetings and names James was too distracted to remember.

The one with the big hair eyed up Jed while sparkly t-shirt girl seemed intent on making eye contact with James.

Maybe they'd discussed things beforehand and agreed on who'd flirt with whom.

Sparkles drained her glass and shot James a smile over its rim, then set it down on the bar in front of him, purposely letting her arm drag across his biceps. "That's another drink gone." She leaned on the bar, invading his personal space with all the force of a small army.

He shifted on his seat, trying not to choke on the scent of her perfume. Judging by the smell, she'd bathed in it.

"I wish that bartender would hurry up," she huffed.

The bartender who'd been scrubbing the spot in front of Jed so vigorously had disappeared once the women had showed up. Now she stood at the other end of the bar, her back to them.

Sparkles lingered at James' side anyway, occasionally looking up and batting her eyelashes at him.

If she thought he was going to buy her a drink, she was barking up the wrong tree.

"So what's your name?" she asked when he said nothing.

It was hard to ignore her when she was right in his face.

"James," he said, because ignoring her didn't seem to be a very effective deterrent anyway.

"So what do you do, *James*?" She drew out his name like it was something exotic. "For a living, I mean."

He muttered something about tattooing and piercing, an answer that had her rambling on about getting inked while raising one sandaled foot. The tattoo she pointed out to him – hoisting her leg so high that half the bar could probably see up her skirt – was a butterfly, right above her ankle. Obviously flash art. Beneath it, the word *princess* was emblazoned in rounded letters.

Done in a lurid shade of pink, it reminded him of the Barbie dolls Crystal had played with when they'd been little.

She didn't seem to notice his lack of enthusiasm. Or at least, she didn't care. She kept talking and gave her eyelids such a workout he almost expected her lashes to start shedding beneath the weight of her heavy-duty mascara.

"Look," he finally said. "I'm just here to have a beer with my friend. I'm not really in the mood for conversation."

She stopped mid-sentence, her eyes going wide.

She looked so stricken, he almost felt bad for hurting her feelings. Almost. All his emotions had been sucked into the black hole Arianna's rejection had created inside him, and he didn't have any to spare on a stranger with a perfume addiction.

"Well," she said, drawing her hand back across the bar and clicking long, neon nails against its surface. "Truth is, I'm not really in the mood for conversation either." She leaned even closer and touched his forearm, dragging one nail across his tattoos. "What do you say we get out of here? Don't worry about your friend – *my* friend will keep him occupied."

Big Hair seemed to be plying all her conversational charms on Jed, who simply shook his head and took another drink.

James moved his arm, shaking off Sparkles' touch. "No thanks."

She pouted for half a second before glaring at him. "Whatever."

Moments later, Sparkles and Big Hair had withdrawn and were stalking across the room, arms linked.

"Thanks," Jed said, turning to James, "for whatever you said to get rid of them. That girl's hairspray fumes were giving me a headache."

James started to take a drink of his half-empty beer, then put it down. Fuck it – he couldn't take this anymore. "I need you to do me a big favor."

Jed put down his drink, too. "What?"

James pulled out his wallet, took out several bills and laid them on the bar in front of Jed. "Give one of these to the bartender and use the others to take a cab home. I've got to go, but I'll try not to be too long. I'll be by your place to pick up Emily in an hour or two."

Jed looked at the bills, then back up at James. "Take the money. You need it to take care of your niece."

James shook his head.

Jed sighed, took the bills and shoved them back into James' hand. "James."

He stood still, though he was itching to leave.

"Remember what I said. Don't sell yourself short."

James left, walking out of the bar, in the same direction Sparkles and Big Hair had gone.

* * * * *

James took a deep breath of night air as he climbed the stairs to Arianna's apartment, cleansing his lungs of the perfume-and-whisky scent that had permeated the bar. Despite the 20 minute drive from there to Arianna's place, the smell lingered, clouding his senses and reminding him why he was there.

Whether Jed had simply wanted to offer James some sympathy and a chance to get outside of his own head, or had had a more complex motivation for inviting him out for a drink, James wasn't sure. Either way, James owed him big time. Him and Sparkles.

Being preyed upon by the girl in the glittering t-shirt had opened up his eyes, forcing him to confront a stark truth. When she'd touched his arm and batted her eyelashes at him, he'd felt absolutely nothing. There'd been a time when he might've accepted the attention, the invitation. Now, he was as capable of doing that as he was of walking through fire, or breathing under water. The idea wasn't just painful; it was unnatural, against the very essence of his nature.

Arianna had changed him. So here he was, ready to tell her that – ready to take Jed's advice and try one more time. Maybe Jed had been right. Maybe he *had* made a habit of thinking he wasn't good enough.

It was a natural consequence of spending most of his life being unwanted, feeling like nothing. When he was confronted with rejection, he relapsed into what had often seemed like an obvious truth: he was flawed. A burden to people who knew better – were better.

Fuck that. He knew now what he could offer Arianna: everything. Everything he was, everything he had. If it wasn't enough for her, fine. But he had to know, had to make sure she knew what he was offering, how he felt about her. How compatible he knew they were, even if she had doubts, for some reason.

He stopped in front of her unit, reading and re-reading the number on the door. Though the flight of steps was short, his heart pounded like he'd been climbing for ages. Taking a deep breath, he reached out and knocked.

There was no answer.

He tried again.

Still nothing.

Arianna was gone.

* * * * *

Arianna had barely finished her first cup of coffee when a knock came at the door. Rising and blinking the last traces of sleep from her eyes, she shuffled to the door. Today would be another day of watching Maya – another challenge. Still, Arianna felt oddly ready to face it, and not just because of the caffeine she'd just inhaled. As she strode out into the living room, she paused to admire the new addition that hung above the couch.

Set in a silver frame, an 8 x 10" print adorned the otherwise bare wall. It was the first picture ever taken of Arianna's daughter – the one where she held her, sitting propped up in the hospital bed.

She'd gone to a 24 hour drug store the night before to scan her original and have an enlarged print made. Now, the picture was where it belonged – not just in a box under her bed. From now on, anyone she trusted enough to allow into her home would be someone she'd be willing to tell about her daughter. After all, she was who she was, and deep down, she was proud of the beautiful girl she'd brought into the world.

No more hiding who she was, no more secrets – if she didn't think a guy might be willing to try to understand her past, she wouldn't bring him home. Period. She'd only invite people into her life if she was willing to take that chance on them.

Just days ago, the thought of hanging Miranda's picture in her living room would've terrified her. But James had changed her, even if she'd lost him. Now she knew that she didn't want to relive the mistake she'd so recently made: getting close to someone she knew she could love and breaking her own heart by hiding who she was.

When she answered the door, she answered it with a smile.

That smile faltered when she saw who stood on the other side. Instead of Selena, James filled the doorway. Arianna's heart launched into a frenzied pace, stunning her into motionless silence.

"I dropped Emily off at day care early this morning," he said. "I need to talk to you. Please."

She couldn't deny him. It'd taken all her willpower to end things between them on the phone. Now, she found herself stepping aside and nodding.

The living room was awash in bright morning light that filtered through the window, plus the illumination shed by the fixture on the ceiling. As James emerged from the hallway's shadows, he looked more tired than ever. The circles beneath his eyes were an unmissable shade of purple, and his tense expression made him seem exhausted, too. He closed the door softly behind himself and met Arianna's eyes.

"I stopped by here last night," he said, "but you weren't home."

"I was out on an errand." She thought of the picture hanging above the couch, but couldn't look away from James. Tired and sad-looking or not, he was a sight for sore eyes. She never would've been able to deny him to his face. Even now, she ached to wrap her arms around him.

He nodded. "I couldn't sleep worth a damn last night, and not because of Emily. All I could think about was you."

Her heart skipped a beat, fueling visions of embracing James. Fact was, her heart didn't know how to protect itself from hurt. She'd spent hours lying awake thinking about him, too.

"I know you said that you don't think what we have is cut out to last, but I think you're wrong. I *know* you're wrong. That's what I came here to tell you. Arianna, I want to be with you. For a while, it sure as hell seemed like you wanted to be with me too. What made you change your mind?"

A knot had formed in her throat. She swallowed it, staring back at him. "I loved all time I spent with you – every hour, every minute. But—"

Another knock came at the door.

"My sister," Arianna said, not sure whether she should be annoyed or relieved that they'd been interrupted. Her heart felt like it was beating a million times per minute; she'd been so close to confessing what she'd kept secret. After all, she'd let James into her home ... there was only one thing to do now, if she was going to keep the promise she'd made to herself.

Selena stepped through the door, Maya in her arms, as soon as Arianna opened it. "Morning," she said. "Maya fell asleep in the car. I don't know if she'll wake up or not. She might just keep napping and—"

Selena stopped in her tracks the moment she laid eyes on James. "Oh. I didn't know anyone else would be here."

If Arianna had been less anxious, she might've been a little amused at her sister's expression of shock. Selena was probably busy assuming that James had spent the night – a reasonable conclusion considering the fact that he'd shown up just after Arianna had finished her morning coffee.

"Selena, this is James. He's the friend I was babysitting for last week. James, this is Selena."

That was all the explanation she offered, even after Selena and James exchanged greetings. She had enough to explain to James without worrying about trying to cram in an explanation of their relationship for Selena's sake. Stepping forward, she took Maya, who was still sleeping, from Selena's arms. "I've got a little bed made up for her in my room. I'll go lay her down."

She retreated to her bedroom and settled Maya on the air mattress she'd layered with a sheet and blanket. When she returned to the living room, Selena was still there, staring openly at James.

She looked a little wary; maybe she was judging him by his tattoos.

In that moment, Arianna couldn't have cared less.

James must've cared. "You mind if I make myself a cup of coffee, Arianna?"

"Of course not. Go ahead."

As soon as he left for the kitchen, Selena turned to Arianna. "I'm normally not into tattoos," she whispered, "but wow – he's cute."

Arianna barely kept her jaw from dropping. Selena's reaction to James had been a surprise… Maybe James would surprise her, too.

She barely dared to hope, but the idea was there.

Arianna was already glancing toward the kitchen when Selena laid a hand on her arm. "I have some news – only Josh, mom and dad know so far."

Arianna turned back to face her sister. "What is it?"

"Well, I just found out last night… I'm pregnant again!" Her voice rose several octaves, echoing throughout the apartment.

"Wow," Arianna said, ignoring the mixed emotions that sailed through her as her mind flashed back to her own pregnancy. "Congratulations. When are you due?"

"I don't know yet," she replied, still speaking loudly. "I have a doctor appointment in a couple days. I didn't even suspect I was pregnant until I started feeling nauseous in the morning. Really tired, too, in the middle of the afternoon. Well, I'm sure you remember exactly how it is."

Arianna flinched, but Selena didn't seem to notice. "My best guess is that I'm somewhere between six and eight weeks along," she said. "Probably not any farther…"

Arianna stood, stiff and nervous as Selena rambled on, a big smile pasted on her face. Was she totally oblivious to what she'd just said? And had James heard?

Selena was talking so loudly, it'd be a wonder if he hadn't. Yeah, Arianna had already decided to reveal her past to him, but it was her secret to tell, not Selena's. What if he was drawing the wrong conclusions as they spoke?

It was a relief when Selena finally left, accepting another feeble round of congratulations from Arianna as she rushed out the door, mumbling something about being late.

When she was finally gone, Arianna retreated to the kitchen, her stomach in knots.

James was standing in front of the counter, taking a deep drink from a steaming cup of coffee. His eyes met hers over the cup's rim, and the steam rising up from its depths did nothing to veil the intensity in his gaze.

"Guess you heard my sister's news." She stood facing him, her nails digging into her palms as nervous sweat began to dampen the back of her neck.

"Yeah. Good for her."

"And ... well, I guess you heard everything."

He nodded.

Arianna's stomach was a mass of knots, and she could feel her pulse beating, radiating throughout her tensed-up body. Telling the truth was even harder than she'd anticipated. Maybe it would get easier with time. After all, what could her future hold that could possibly hurt more than what she'd endured in her past, or James rejecting her?

"I was pregnant once," she said. "I had a baby."

CHAPTER 12

For a long time, James was silent. Half hidden by his coffee cup, his face was unreadable. When he spoke, his voice was surprisingly soft. "Did something happen to it ... the baby, I mean?"

Arianna shook her head, horrified at the sudden pressure that welled up behind her eyes. "No, no – nothing like that. She was fine – *is* fine. She was adopted just after birth."

Adrenaline flooded Arianna's system, filling her mouth with a coppery taste as she waited for his reaction.

When he said nothing, her fears were confirmed. She'd expected him to lash out at her, but if he was too disgusted to respond at all ... well, that was even worse.

"Now you know why we're not compatible," she said.

He set his coffee cup down on the counter and straightened, eyes still locked with hers. "Why?"

Why had she given her daughter up for adoption? A million reasons...

"I was only 16. The father wasn't much older than I was and dumped me a few days after I told him I was pregnant.

166

Said I should have an abortion, and that it was my problem if I did something stupid like choose to have the baby…" She shook her head, shame creeping over her as she thought back to how stupid she'd been to ever be with such a loser. Sure, she'd only been a teenager, but still…

She hated that she'd once been naïve enough to actually think Cody had loved her. Looking back on it, she felt cheated in the worst way – manipulated into taking risks he hadn't been willing to take with her, when it really came down to it. Nothing had ever made her feel so stupid as that one-sided love.

"I never could've afforded to take care of her. I lived in a two bedroom house with my parents, sharing a room with my sister. I was only a sophomore in highschool. I—"

"No." James shook his head. "Not that. I mean, why aren't we compatible?"

Arianna blinked, unnerved by the moisture that clung to her eyelashes. "I gave up my baby. She's 10 now and has been raised by another couple – strangers – her whole life. I know how you feel about your sister … about parents who don't take care of their children."

"Arianna." He frowned. "You're not like my sister. For fuck's sake… I'd never think that about you. And if you were only 16, maybe letting a stable couple adopt your baby *was* taking care of her."

For several long moments, Arianna said nothing – did nothing. James' words washed over her and through her like an electric shock. She'd expected to have to explain – argue, even – if she was going to have even the smallest chance at making him see the truth: that giving up her child had been agony, and that she'd truly done it out of love.

It'd been her way of righting the wrongs that had led to her pregnancy in the first place, her way of giving her child what she'd always craved: unconditional love, the experience of being the center of someone's universe. Was it really possible that he already understood … that she'd almost ruined everything for nothing?

"I didn't think you'd see it that way." Her voice was barely above a whisper.

"You thought I'd look down on you?"

She nodded.

He swore. "The state took me and my sister away from our parents when I was seven and she was five. I went into my first grade classroom one day with a broken nose, and the school guidance counselor got the story out of me." He tapped a finger against the bridge of his nose, where a small bump was still visible.

"The drugs, the neglect and the abuse… Everything was so shitty at home, but Crystal and I were still afraid to leave. They took us anyway, of course, and by that time, we weren't lovable little babies. We ended up staying foster kids until we hit 18. And you know what? Some of the foster parents we stayed with weren't much better than our real parents. And none of them wanted us for very long. Most of the time, Crystal and I didn't even live with the same family."

"I'm sorry," Arianna said, her gut wrenching as she imagined James as a small child, hair bright as gold, face streaming with blood.

He shrugged. "It's in the past now. Point is, I wish my mom had done what you did, Arianna. Given us up when we were born, let us have a chance with a real family. That would've been… That could've changed everything. But not everybody cares about their kids enough to do what's best for them.

"I'm not saying you ever would've used drugs or hurt your baby or anything like that," he continued. "But you let her be adopted because you thought she'd have a better life that way, right?"

Arianna nodded. How could she possibly explain that once she got to the hospital, the decision that'd seemed so logical had ended up tearing her apart? Her own love for her baby combined with surging hormones had created an instant bond that'd been excruciating to destroy. The birth had hurt, physically – afterward she'd been left bruised and bleeding, stitched back together in places so tender it'd been hell just to sit. But none of that had hurt a fraction as much as handing Miranda over to Joy and Dave.

"I don't see anything wrong with that," James said.

The pressure behind her eyes reached breaking point as she realized that she didn't have to explain. James was already on her side. It'd been so long since she'd had anyone who hadn't tried to shame her over being a teen mother…

"I'm sorry," she said as a tear slipped free and burnt a trail down her cheek. "I misjudged you."

"Give me a chance to prove myself," he said. "That's all I'm asking. Let's do this a while longer. We're right for each other; you'll see that."

She shook her head. "You've already proven yourself. I was just afraid… I was sure you'd reject me when you found out about my baby, and I couldn't stand the thought."

He crossed the tiny kitchen, and before she could draw another breath, he wrapped his arms around her.

If she'd had any air in her lungs, she would've lost it right then and there. Instead, she breathed deeply, inhaling his scent. It was even better than the coffee aroma that lingered in the air.

They sealed the moment with a kiss that made her heart race. She leaned into it, but as his hands settled on her hips, a small sound came from her bedroom.

The giggle was enough to have them pulling reluctantly apart, letting a little distance separate their bodies. To say that Maya was mobile was an understatement, and that reality drove thoughts of using the kitchen table creatively from Arianna's mind. "I'd better go make sure she's not trying to climb my bookshelf again."

When Arianna reached her bedroom, she found Maya curled on her little bed, smiling in her sleep. Still, the nap probably wouldn't last much longer. Returning to the kitchen, Arianna pressed a kiss against James' jaw, ending it sooner than she really wanted to. There was no way the gesture could convey everything she felt: the overwhelming sense of relief and rightness, the desire that was more intense than ever.

"Sorry my babysitting is putting a damper on our alone time," she said. It was so rare for him to have time without Emily, it seemed too bad that he and Arianna weren't free to spend it how they'd like.

"Doesn't matter," he said, his voice a little rough. "I want you, but it doesn't matter. All I care about is that you want me too."

A tremor raced through her, causing everything inside her to draw up tight for one breathtaking moment. "I definitely do."

Silence stretched between them, fraught with temptation. "Here," she eventually said, taking his hand and leading him out of the kitchen, "I have something to show you."

They stopped in the living room, and she nodded at the picture hanging above her couch. "Her name's Miranda."

A sense of relief rushed through her, even before James replied. She'd kept her promise to herself, and it felt ... right. The weight of keeping her secret was gone, replaced by the satisfaction of having someone to share it with.

"Do you have any other pictures?" he asked. "Do her parents send you any or anything like that?"

"Yeah. Every year, on her birthday. Do you want to see?"

"Yeah."

She retrieved the heart-shaped box from under her bed, vowing to find a better place to keep it. When she returned to the living room, she settled down onto the couch with James, and he wrapped an arm around her as she lifted the lid.

* * * * *

"When I came to you for my first tattoo, I was kind of worried," Arianna said, shivering as James' fingertips skimmed her hip, tracing the colorful design there. "I thought you might see my stretch marks and realize that I'd had a baby." She bit her tongue, stifling a gasp as his touch slipped below. "I didn't think we'd ever end up seeing each other outside of Hot Ink, of course, but I was still nervous that you might ask."

As he lay stretched beside her on her bed, he shrugged, his bare shoulders rising and falling. "A lot of the women I tattoo have them, and yours are so faint – the kind that could be just from growing, not necessarily from pregnancy. I didn't think anything of it."

The marks striped her hips, pale white lines against darker skin. "Well, I noticed them every time I caught a glimpse of myself in the mirror after showering in the morning. They reminded me of everything that had happened, and it hurt. That's why I wanted to get a tattoo on my hip, so I'd see something pretty when I looked at myself there."

He made a sound deep in his throat. "You were pretty without any ink there. But yeah … the tattoo looks pretty damn good, if I do say so myself."

He moved before she could say another word, sliding down the bed, his naked body slipping against the sheets.

When he pressed his lips to the tattoo in question, her entire body tingled.

"I was a little worried when you came to me for your first tattoo too," he said, raising his head enough to meet her eyes. His breath streamed hot over her hip, her pussy, tempting her to wriggle in search of more direct contact.

"Why?" she asked.

"I was afraid you'd realize I wanted to do this." He lowered his head between her thighs, pressing his mouth full-on against her sensitive skin.

She did more than wriggle then – she writhed. "Really?"

He nodded, drawing his tongue over her clit before meeting her gaze again. "I remember it like it was yesterday. The way you sat in my chair with your jeans unbuttoned and unzipped… I could see your panties. They were purple, and I wanted to rip them off you." He brushed his lips lightly against her mound. "Thought about it the whole time. I know it's unprofessional as hell, but… Can you blame me?"

A breathless laugh escaped her as secret pleasure unfolded inside her. He remembered what color panties she'd been wearing? That'd been almost a year ago… "No. I might've had a few of those sort of thoughts myself."

"Oh yeah?" His breath was still rushing over her skin, teasing.

She nodded. "Yeah."

"If I'd known that, I would've made my move a long time ago. You were hard to read, though. Figured if you knew just touching you made me hard, you might never come back."

His words inspired a wave of what-ifs, along with another shiver. Had they missed out on nearly a year they could've spent together?

Maybe, maybe not. There was no telling how things might've worked out under different circumstances. "I'm glad we're together now."

"Me too."

He stopped teasing her then, applying his tongue to her clit with a clear, singular purpose. The slide of it against her sensitive skin was perfect, each stroke building on the last, pushing her close to the climaxes that came so easily when she was with him. His touch dispelled every past disappointment, showing her what she'd missed out on for the first 26 years of her life.

No one had ever cared enough to touch her like he did – as if his pleasure depended on hers.

She'd made some bad decisions in the past, mostly out of ignorance. That was over now. James was one good decision she planned to stick with. Forever, if he was up for it. Reaching down, she buried her hands in his hair.

He moaned as she closed her fists, knuckles going white. His hair was short, but still long enough to hold on to.

She came with his tongue against her clit, his hands on her thighs, fingertips denting her skin deeply as he held her steady. The climax hit her hard, building up to a breathtaking peak and then spiraling down, until her bones felt like jelly.

His cock slid up her inner leg, stiff and thick, as he settled between her thighs. He surprised her by rolling over, pulling her on top of him.

Still a little shaky, she braced herself with a hand on his chest. A swallow's wing peeked from between her fingers, dark ink that stood out boldly beneath a haze of golden chest hair. "Did you get these at Hot Ink?" she asked.

He nodded. "From Jed."

"I like them." She traced the contour of one bird's delicate body. The design was classic and looked good against his classically masculine frame, all lean muscles, dark ink and just enough hair. "Why'd you choose this design?"

There were personal reasons behind all her own tattoos – a fact that made her deeply curious about his ink, especially the tattoos on his chest, which stood out the most.

He shrugged, muscles rippling beneath her palm and splayed fingers. "Sailors used to get them, back in the day. They said that if you died at sea, the swallows would fly down and retrieve your soul, take it to heaven. That stuck with me after I heard it. Guess I liked the idea of something coming down and lifting you out of a dark place, even after you think everything is over."

Arianna's mind flooded with images of the sea, vast and crushing, a dark place where people had been lost forever. "That is nice."

"I got them a few months after I started my apprenticeship. Working at Hot Ink – having something I cared about – seemed a lot like being lifted out of a dark place."

His confession fueled her curiosity. "What did you do before then?"

"Bounced around between a few different construction gigs. Nothing too skilled, because I didn't know shit about anything. Just the kind of work that makes you feel like you've been run over by a truck at the end of the day."

It was kind of hot to imagine him sweating and hauling around heavy stuff, though she liked the idea of him bent over her with a tattoo machine better. "Not exactly the most fulfilling job, I guess." Seeing his art displayed permanently on living canvasses had to be more satisfying.

"No. I like it at Hot Ink a lot better – the work, the people. It's kind of like a family."

His mention of Hot Ink made her think of her time there – time spent with his hands and eyes on her body. That contact had inspired thoughts of how they lay now – him on his back, muscled body against the sheets, with her straddling his hips. His cock pressed against her from below, the naked flesh hard and hot against her pussy.

"There are condoms in my pocket," he said, following her gaze, then tipping his head toward his jeans, which lay abandoned beside him. "Put one on me so I can be inside you." The conversational tone had left his voice, replaced by a scraping note of desire.

She reached for his jeans, found one and opened it. Pinching the tip above the head of his dick, she rolled the rest down his shaft, stopping at the base, her fingertips brushing the captive bead there. The sensation of the steel against her skin was a turn on, even if it was only her hand.

He was inside her a moment later, thrusting up as she sank down. He went deeper than she'd expected, despite the fact that she'd just felt her way down every inch of his shaft. For a second, she couldn't breathe.

But her body was made for it, stretching and translating the shock to pleasure. As he rocked into her again, she sighed. This was everything she wanted. Not just the sex, but the closeness – physical and otherwise. There were no secrets between them, and she knew he wouldn't leave her bed until morning. The satisfaction threatened to overwhelm her, almost as intense as her recent orgasm.

James' voice called her back to the present, and she blinked away the haze of bliss so she could meet his eyes. "Thought of this, too," he said. "Just about as soon as I laid eyes on you."

Everything inside her drew up tight. She'd be a liar if she said she hadn't imagined something similar when she'd first met him, though at that point she wouldn't have thought it'd ever become reality. Her reply was a gasp, an involuntary response to the way he thrust hard into her to punctuate his claim.

"Thought of a lot of things, actually. I think it'll take us damn near a month to try everything I imagined within the first hour of laying hands on you."

"Sounds promising," she breathed. "I'm going to hold you to that." She rocked back against him, seeking the friction of his piercing against her clit.

He sighed, running a hand up her side and cupping one of her breasts. His fingers slipped over her nipple, then drew deliberately back, teasing it to a stiff peak. He slipped his other hand between her thighs and touched her clit, beginning a steady rhythm that drew another climax from her.

It was even better than the first. Although coming against his open mouth was undeniably erotic, nothing compared to having an orgasm while he was inside her. His cock gave her body something to tighten around, something to squeeze. Her head swam as it did just that, his pleasure spiking every time he finished a stroke, reaching a place deep inside her.

When it was over, her thigh muscles ached – fiercely, but not in a bad way. She stopped rocking against him.

He wrapped an arm around her waist and pulled her down, so that she lay flat on top of him. Like that, she could feel his heartbeat, the rhythm of his breathing. And then there was the solid presence of him inside her, a firmness in her core that marked each moment with pleasure. When he moved beneath her, simultaneously wrapping a hand in her hair, the moan that rose from deep in her chest was automatic.

He held her like that for a while, one arm crossing her body and his fingers tangled, knuckles brushing her skull while he maintained a steadily-increasing rhythm below. With her on top, he went faster and deeper than he had when it'd been the other way around. By the time he came, it would've been hard for her to endure it if she'd still been riding him, her back straight. But with him holding her close, she didn't just endure it; she savored each moment of the intensity.

Even after he was finished, he didn't let go of her. They still lay chest to chest, hearts beating against each other's. Later, after he finally pulled out, they reentwined and slept in a similar position. He got up a couple times to take care of Emily when she woke up, but he always came back.

It was the best night of Arianna's life, and the really amazing part was knowing that she'd have plenty more just like it.

* * * * *

7 Years Ago

"You know we open in 20 minutes, right?" James stood in the doorway of Jed's apartment above Hot Ink. Below, the shop was empty. Tyler wouldn't be showing up until around three.

"Yeah." Jed stood at the stove with his back to James. He'd dressed himself in jeans and a t-shirt, but his hair looked like he hadn't touched it in days. Months ago, he'd shaved it all off – for Alice – but it had grown back in and was just long enough to make him look crazy. He had a bad cowlick on the back of his head, and the rest of his hair stuck up at weird angles too, begging for a comb.

"I'll be down in a little while," Jed said. "I'm making some chili. Gotta finish it – can't leave it to burn."

So that explained the scorched-pepper and onion scented fog that was making James' eyes water. "What's the chili for?"

"To eat." Jed stood there stirring the pot, still not facing James. "Don't order anything for lunch today – you can have some of this."

James bit his tongue as the kitchen air scorched his lungs. "I didn't know you cooked."

Jed shrugged and pointed to a lone takeout container that sat open on the counter. "Ate some bad Chinese last night. You don't want to know what happened afterward, trust me. Figured it was time to get my head out of my ass and learn how to make something for myself."

"So the recipe then ... it's one of Alice's?" Saying her name felt like stepping on broken glass, hoping it wouldn't crumble beneath his weight.

"Nah. She was too good of a cook ... I needed something simple. Got this off the internet."

James let his gaze rove over the kitchen, taking in all the signs that marked it as Alice's domain: the decorative canisters lining the counter and the brightly-colored spoons hanging on a rack above the stove, the tea tins and patterned kitchen towels. It didn't seem like she could possibly be gone from a place that was so clearly hers, but Jed — disheveled and trying to make the place his, out of necessity — proved that she was. The signs of his attempted takeover were there too: coffee grounds spilled on the counter, dirty knives and a pile of chopped-up vegetables that looked like mangled confetti.

"You want some help?" James offered. He didn't know shit about cooking, but neither did Jed, so what could it hurt?

"No." Jed dumped the mess of mystery-vegetables into the pot. "I can do this."

"Okay man. But just so you know ... you look like shit. No offense, but you might want to run a comb through your hair or something before you come downstairs."

He didn't want anyone else to see Jed as he really was: broken from the inside out, now that Alice was gone. It just seemed wrong, somehow. Like if he really cared, he'd help Jed protect that side of himself that was so at odds with the rest of him: the unshakable, driven person James had met when he'd first walked through Hot Ink's doors. The man who'd been master of his own domain, completely at home in the business he'd built from the ground up...

Of course, now James saw that Alice had been half of all that, half of the force behind Hot Ink and half of Jed, when it came down to it. But she was gone and James knew the last thing she would've wanted would be for Jed to let it all fall apart.

"Tell me the truth," Jed said as he dumped a shitload of red powder into the chili pot, "do I look like some crazy bastard who should be living on top of a mountain?"

"Turn around," James replied.

Jed did, exposing a jaw darkened and roughened by stubble that was almost thick enough to be a full-blown beard.

"Yeah," James said, "that about sums it up. I didn't know you were so self-aware."

Jed turned back around. "Alice always said I looked like a mountain man when I went too long without shaving."

"She was right."

"Some days I think I'd rather live alone and batshit crazy on the side of some mountain than wake up here and not see her in our home. Our shop. Without her it's just … not right. Not fucking right at all."

"Yeah, I know," James said, because he did and because he knew saying otherwise wouldn't lessen Jed's pain. "Your first appointment is in 10 minutes. Should I tell your client you're lost somewhere in the mountains?"

"Nah. I'm coming down. Thanks."

"No problem." James didn't ask what he was being thanked for. He didn't need to; his time at Hot Ink had already taught him what he'd always suspected, which was that it was better not to be alone. No matter how bad things were, having a place to be and people to be with made it better, at least by a little.

* * * * *

As the best man, James had an up-close view of Jed and Karen's wedding ceremony. And he had to admit, it was more than worth having been cornered and lassoed with a measuring tape over.

Karen looked beautiful, and Jed looked better than he ever had. More importantly, they both looked really happy.

Everyone knew Karen was a perfectionist when it came to photos and had bent over backwards to plan her wedding in time to have a certain photographer present at the ceremony. Still, it was like she didn't even notice the click or flash of perfect, expensive photos being captured as she and Jed stood holding hands.

They exchanged vows they'd written themselves, and then rings. James could remember the last time Jed had worn a golden band, and those memories underlaid the new ones being forged just a few feet from him.

No man was an island, that was for sure. The threads that tied everyone in the small chapel together were many and multi-faceted. In the audience, there were husbands and wives, brothers and sisters. Friends and colleagues, too. Lots of people who all mattered to each other in lots of different ways.

And then there was Arianna. James couldn't help but look at her sitting in the second row of chairs, holding Emily in her lap. And it occurred to him that she'd made herself an island – or at least tried to – for way too long. The past had cut her deep and though she gave selflessly to people like him, Emily and even her sister, who didn't treat her that well, it seemed like nobody had given back to her in a long time.

He knew she hadn't wanted that. He knew because he'd been alone for a long time and had hated it, even though he hadn't known what to do to change things. Now, he loved her and wanted to give her everything, including the ties he shared with the people who filled the room. He wanted her forever, and he wanted her to be happy. Finally, it no longer felt like those two things had to be mutually exclusive.

* * * * *

"Don't tell her I told you this," James said, speaking softly into Arianna's ear, "but Karen told me she's going to throw her bouquet at you."

"*At* me?" Arianna sat a little straighter in her seat at a dining table in the reception hall, glancing around in search of the bride.

Karen was several yards away, posing for a picture with her maid of honor, Mina, and Mina's little sister.

James nodded. "I was the last one at Hot Ink to get into a serious relationship, so she figures she needs to do everything she can to make sure I don't go back to being the only single one. That's what Jed says, anyway – he warned me about the bouquet thing. When Karen tosses it, she's going to try to make sure it goes right into your hands."

Arianna let her gaze rove over James for the millionth time that day. He looked perfect in his tux, and the way the tattoos on his hands peeked out from beneath the cuffs of his sleeves was hot as hell. "You can tell Karen not to worry – I don't plan to let you go back to being the only single one."

He smiled, but before he could say anything, Emily piped up. Now more than two months old, she'd recently discovered her voice and had gotten into the habit of cooing when she wanted to be heard.

"Make sure you hand her over to me before the bouquet toss," James said. "I wouldn't want her to get hit by the flowers."

Arianna picked up one of the wedding favors from the table – a tulle satchel full of chocolates – and dangled it in front of Emily. The shiny candy wrappers glistened as the bag spun, and the baby batted at the makeshift toy with one chubby fist.

"Deal," Arianna said. "But consider yourself warned: the fact that I won't be holding a baby means that I'll have my hands free to catch the bouquet. And if Karen will be aiming at me…"

"Catch away," James said, straightening the hem of Emily's frilly, glittery dress. "I'm not afraid. And it'll make Karen's day."

Arianna wasn't so sure about that. Judging by the way Karen looked at Jed as she glided across the room to press a kiss against his jaw, nothing could possibly make her day better. Still, if James didn't have any qualms about Arianna catching a fated bouquet, neither did she. There were much harsher realities to contemplate than a lifetime spent with him.

"You guys!" Karen looked away from her new husband long enough to wave in James and Arianna's direction. "Come on. We're doing a group photo with everyone from Hot Ink."

James stood while Arianna remained seated, the baby squirming in her lap.

"You too, Arianna," Karen said. "You're a loyal client, after all." As Arianna followed James, she thought she heard Karen mutter something along the lines of 'and you're practically family too', but it was hard to tell for sure.

"Mallory and Sam, come on," Karen urged, motioning toward a woman with sable curls and a tall, muscular guy with reddish hair. "And Jess, no way are you getting out of this photo. Hot Ink clients love your artwork."

By the time Karen had finished summoning people, nearly a third of the wedding guests were gathered for a photo. Shoulders and elbows rubbed together, but everyone seemed happy. Even Emily smiled as the flash bathed the group in white light.

"I'll make sure everyone gets a copy of the best one," Karen said after the photographer had taken several more photos.

As the group broke up into smaller segments, dividing naturally as people got caught up in conversation with one another, James turned to Arianna. "Let's get one of us together." He tipped his head toward the photographer.

"Turn the baby so her face will be in the picture," the woman behind the camera said. "This will be a great family photo – you all look so nice."

A little heat crept into Arianna's cheeks as she complied, trying to position Emily at the best possible angle as James wrapped an arm around her waist. Neither of them bothered correcting the photographer, and Arianna leaned lightly against James as her mind whirled with images of what a future with him might bring.

Maybe someday they'd be a family for real. James had grown up without one, and although Arianna loved her parents and sister, the bonds she shared with them weren't as strong as she would've liked. Unlike when she was around them, she never felt judged with James, and didn't doubt the depth of his affection. He was exactly the sort of person she could imagine spending the rest of her life with.

"I'll make sure Karen gets us a couple copies of that," James said when the photographer turned to photograph another couple instead. "I want one for my place, and it'd look great in your living room, next to your picture of you and Miranda."

His words made her smile. "Yeah, it would."

"Hey, look." He nodded to the left. "I think Karen's getting ready to toss her bouquet."

Sure enough, Karen was motioning to many of the women present. Mallory and Jess drew close to her, as did several other women whose names Arianna didn't know. No sooner had Arianna laid eyes on the bride than Karen motioned toward her, smiling brightly.

"Watch out for Mallory," James said. "I think she'll be your fiercest competition – she and Tyler are already engaged."

"You sound like you're counting on me to catch this bouquet," Arianna teased as she handed over Emily.

"I am." He smiled, but his gaze was intense as it locked with hers. "Catch it, and your fate is sealed – you're mine forever."

Arianna opened and closed her hands, imagining the feel of rose stems against her palm, the sensation of a ring sliding onto her finger – the beginning of forever. "Mallory doesn't stand a chance."

James grinned.

She smiled back and hurried toward the bride, her eyes on the dozen roses she held, bound together with white ribbon. When she joined the other women, she glanced over her shoulder at James, unable to help thinking how good a golden band would look on his left ring finger, shining bright below the dark ink that marked his hands.

Forever couldn't come soon enough.

EPILOGUE

It wasn't a surprise when Crystal walked through James' apartment door – she'd called ahead of time to let him know she was on her way. The sight of her still had him on edge though, torn between anger and relief. Finally, she'd come back for her daughter – now if only he knew she could be trusted to care for four month old Emily.

"Hey." She stood in his living room, looking the same as ever. Long, straight blonde hair and green eyes, a slender build that made her look even younger than she really was. James had to admit, she looked good – not like a junkie. Hopefully, hers wasn't a case of deceiving appearances.

"Hey."

"Where's Emily?" Crystal rocked up onto her toes, craning her neck to look around the apartment.

As if on cue, Arianna emerged from James' bedroom, cradling the infant against her chest. Emily was freshly changed and wearing a clean pair of pajamas she'd needed after spitting up on the last ones.

"You must be Crystal," Arianna said as James' sister rushed forward and scooped the baby from her arms.

"Yeah. And you're…"

"Arianna is my girlfriend," James said.

Crystal held Emily tight, like she'd been separated from her by some circumstance beyond her control. James had to bite his tongue, though at least Crystal was happy to see her kid. That was more than he could ever have said about his and Crystal's mom.

"Oh." Crystal barely spared Arianna another glance, appearing absorbed in her baby instead. "Wow, she's gotten so big… Thanks for taking care of her for me, James."

"Arianna deserves just as much thanks as I do. I have a job you know, and I couldn't afford to keep her in day care all the time. Arianna's been watching her a couple days every week."

Crystal took a longer look at Arianna this time. James braced himself for what she might say. If she complained… His jaw ached from the tension. Crystal had sacrificed any right to complain about anything when it came to Emily the day she'd abandoned her.

"Thank you," was all Crystal said.

The stunted conversation slipped into silence, the quiet broken only by the occasional coo from Emily.

"Well, you don't have to worry about day care and stuff anymore," Crystal eventually said. "And if you tell me how much you spent on it, I'll pay you back over time once I get a job. It'll probably take a while, but…"

"Do you have a job lined up?" James asked.

Crystal shook her head.

"What about a place to live?"

"No. I've been searching the classifieds for jobs and apartments. I'm planning to take whatever I can get."

James sighed. "You know I'm not going to just let you walk out of here with Emily, right?"

Crystal froze. "What do you mean?"

"You can't just leave with her. You don't have a job – you don't even have a place to live. You just got out of rehab, for fuck's sake. What were you planning to do, live in your car?" He'd done it before, and it wasn't something he'd let Emily endure for even a minute. For that matter, he didn't want his sister to go through it either, no matter what she'd done.

"I thought maybe I could stay in a motel until I find something else. I have a little bit of money." She bit her lip. "A really little bit."

James swore. "You're not whisking Emily away to some fleabag motel. And even when you do find an apartment and a job, you're not taking her until you're ready to take care of her."

"She's my baby!"

"Yeah, well you abandoned her. Don't try to play the concerned mother card now – you left her hungry and alone on my doorstep."

Crystal's eyes grew doubly bright with unshed tears, a familiar sight from their lousy childhoods. "He wasn't supposed to leave her like that! He promised me he'd give her to you. He was never supposed to leave her side until you had her. He promised."

"That's what happens when you trust a shitbag junkie. Was he the father?"

Crystal shook her head. "Just a friend. I paid him almost everything I had to get him to drive here from Philly and drop her off with you. The father left a long time ago – I don't know where he is."

"Emily shouldn't have had to suffer because you do a shitty job of choosing your friends and boyfriends."

She was silent for a moment. "I know. I know… But I had to get clean. I couldn't think of what else to do. I knew we'd fight if I dropped her off myself, and I was afraid you'd say no. I thought… I had to leave you with no choice. It was the only way I could be sure you'd do it."

"You should've made getting clean a priority when you found out you were pregnant." He couldn't stop throwing the criticisms at her. Every furious thought he'd had over the past three months raced through his mind, creating a whirlwind of accusations. Watching Crystal cradle Emily just made it worse – that was how it should've been from the beginning. That was how it always should've been.

"I did." She stood as straight as she could while holding the baby, tossing her long sheet of fair hair over her shoulder. "When I found out I was pregnant, I stopped using. It was hard, but I did it. Before then it was pills. Sometimes other stuff, if it was around. You know, at parties and things like that. Mostly pills, though. Those were the only thing I was ever hooked on."

"So what was the deal with rehab, then?"

"When Emily was born, they prescribed me pills like the ones I used to take. For the pain from my episiotomy… I tried not to take them at first, but everything hurt. I couldn't even sit without crying. And I was so depressed. The father was gone, and none of my friends wanted to help. I was just … alone.

"Taking the pills made me feel good. Like I could handle everything. You don't understand what it's like, to have all the stress and pain just melt away… To be happy, even when you shouldn't be. I know this sounds shitty, but the times when I was high were the only times I felt like a good mother. It didn't seem like a big deal, until my prescription ran out."

Tears were rolling down her cheeks now, silent but heavy.

James said nothing.

"When that happened, I was desperate. I felt like I had to have them, or I'd just fall apart. When I didn't have any pills in the cabinet, it was like I was lost at sea with no land in sight.

"So I started buying them again – illegally – and my money ran out fast. The utility companies started threatening to shut off my electricity, my water, just a few weeks after I got out of the hospital. I couldn't let that happen. Not with a baby in the house. But I couldn't stop spending everything I got on the pills. I knew I was going to wreck my life and Emily's if I didn't do something.

"I didn't want to end up like our mom. And I didn't want Emily to end up like us. I thought about it and thought about it… Leaving her with you while I got my shit straight was my only option. I'm sorry if that messed things up for you, but I'm not sorry I did it. This was the only way I could give Emily a good life. If there's ever anything I can do to pay you back, I'll do it. I promise."

James shook his head. "Don't worry about paying me back. You don't owe me anything – you owe your daughter everything. Just don't ever touch that shit again."

"I'm not going to. My head is clear now; I just need to get on my feet financially."

"Don't go back to Philly." The last thing she needed was to live in the shadow of her old life, surrounded by the sort of people who'd tempt her to fall back into the trap of substance abuse. And no way was he going to hand over Emily and let Crystal take her away to another city, where he wouldn't be able to check on her. "Stay here."

Crystal nodded. "I need a fresh start. I don't care about Philly; it was just where I ended up. Nobody I knew there gave a shit about me when I really needed them, anyway. Pittsburgh is as good a place as any."

"I mean stay here, at my place. You'll have to sleep on the couch or set up a bed in the living room or something, but I'm not letting Emily go anywhere. Not this soon. You're going to have to prove you'll take good care of her before you leave with her."

Crystal met James' gaze, her eyes rimmed with wetness. It seemed like she might argue, but eventually she nodded. "Thanks. I'd be screwed without you."

It might not have been the most eloquent thing he'd ever heard, but she sounded like she meant it. Somewhere inside James, a weight shifted, and he felt a little lighter. Finally, there was light at the end of the tunnel. Maybe Crystal hadn't fucked up her and Emily's lives so badly after all.

"You'll need help, taking care of a baby. I don't know what I would've done without Arianna, these past few months. Do you have any stuff you need help bringing in out of your car?"

Crystal shook her head. "I'll get it myself." She held Emily a few minutes longer before handing her over to James and exiting the apartment.

James turned to Arianna. "I know it'll be weird with my sister living here, but—"

"Don't worry about it. We can always go to my place when we want privacy. I think it's great that you're helping her and Emily. Nobody deserves to be left all alone to raise a baby." She nodded toward Emily. "I wouldn't want today to be the last time I saw her, either. I'd always wonder how she was doing."

"Yeah. This way, I'll always know she's all right. And as long as Crystal keeps her shit straight, eventually I'll have this place to myself again. Might be a while, though."

"Don't feel like you have to rush them out because of me. Like I said, we'll have my apartment for when we want to be alone."

He shrugged. "It's just that I figure when they're on their feet, you and I could move in together."

A split second of silence followed, and he could've heard a pin drop. It was the first time he'd really brought it up, even though every time he made love to Arianna, she swore she'd be his forever. He was pretty sure she meant it, though sometimes a hint of doubt crept in, a leftover of who he'd been before he'd met her.

"I'd like that," she said, her voice soft but her gaze intense as it met his. "A lot."

Relief crashed down on him with all the force of a tidal wave. "Yeah well, you caught that bouquet at Jed and Karen's wedding, so you don't have much of a choice, do you?"

She smiled. "No, I don't – my fate is sealed."

He motioned toward the baby in his arms. "Years from now we'll have a family of our own, and we can leave our kids with Aunt Crystal some nights so we can go out on hot dates. If she gives us any crap about it, I'll just remind her that she promised to pay me back for watching Emily."

Her smile reached the corners of her eyes now. "I'd like that too. But you know, we could always tell her we were going out and secretly stay *in* together. I think I'd like that even more."

"That's why I love you."

"Really?"

"No. Really, it's just one reason. One out of a million."

"I love you too. And for the record, that bouquet doesn't have anything to do with why. Flowers or not, you were right: we're right for each other."

Ink is forever. So is love.

Stay up to date with the entire Inked in the Steel City Series by visiting the Inked in the Steel City page at ranaerose.com anytime.

Previous titles in the series…

Hot Ink (Inked in the Steel City, #1)

Innocent Ink (Inked in the Steel City, #2)

Dedicated Ink (Inked in the Steel City, #3)

Abiding Ink (Inked in the Steel City, #4)

Serious Ink (Inked in the Steel City, #5)

ABOUT THE AUTHOR

Ranae Rose is the best-selling author of more than twenty adult romances and counting. She calls the US East Coast home and resides there with her family, German Shepherd dogs and overflowing bookshelves. Writing and reading are lifelong passions that consume most of her time, and she's always working on bringing her latest love story idea to life for readers.

www.ranaerose.com

Made in the USA
Middletown, DE
19 April 2015